LOVE BEYOND WORDS

BOOK 9 OF MORNA'S LEGACY SERIES

BETHANY CLAIRE

Editor: Dj Hendrickson
Cover Designed by Damonza

Available In eBook, Paperback, & Hardback

eBook ISBN: 978-0-9978610-2-0
Paperback ISBN: 978-0-9978610-3-7
Hardback ISBN: 978-1-947731-53-0

http://www.bethanyclaire.com

For Elizabeth, Johnetta, Karen, & Vivian

I couldn't do it without you.

CHAPTER 1

*B*oston, Massachusetts—*Present Day*

"*Y*ou're going to be late if you don't hurry up and leave, Laurel. Please don't sabotage this date before it even begins."

"This *date*," I placed as much snark into my tone as I possibly could as I answered her, "wasn't my idea. I can't pretend to be excited about it."

Kate didn't seem at all bothered by my bad attitude.

"Are you seriously still mad at me about the dating profile? You have to admit that I did a fantastic job writing it. I picked only the best photos of you, and…" she waited, leaving a pregnant pause while I stared at her. "It's taken someone who had previously gone three years without a single date and turned her into someone who has gone on ten dates in the last three months."

"Ten first dates in the last three months and every single one of them was awful. I'm not sure we can call that a win."

Scooting herself from her seated position on the couch so she could look back at me, she smiled.

"Okay, I'll admit that none of them were stellar and there were definitely a few weirdos in the mix, but that doesn't mean this date will be bad."

"It's just a feeling I have."

"You always have that feeling. Tell me, how does someone who writes romance novels for a living have such a blatant dislike for all men? It seems to me that would be counterproductive to what you do."

I didn't want to admit that she was right, but since my fallout with the one man I'd thought hung the moon since elementary school, I certainly hadn't seen many examples of great men.

"I don't dislike *all* men. It's just that I seem to come across more rotten men than good ones. And it's called compartmentalizing. People across all professions practice it every single day. If we all had to believe in what we do for a living, the workforce would cease to exist."

My sister's smile dropped as she closed her eyes and shook her head at me.

"Jesus, Laurel, that's the most depressing thing you've ever said. Have you ever considered that your attitude may be the reason why you never seem to stumble across any good men? The law of attraction is real, big sis. Maybe your attitude is just scaring them off. Your vibes are toxic."

She lifted both arms and flailed them around as if to clear the air of my toxicity. The stump on her right arm and the burns over her left hand caused my heart to squeeze painfully in my chest and in an instant I gained a perspective that riddled me with guilt for what a complete and ungrateful snob I was.

All my sister wanted was for me to have something that she believed she could no longer ever have. And while I knew she was wrong—her beauty could hardly be marred by injury—I understood her need to fill her empty schedule with something that made her feel useful. She would happily trade me each of these terrible dates, if she felt she could.

Blushing in embarrassment and shame, I walked around to the front of the couch and sat down next to her.

"You're right. It's not fair of me to judge each of these guys before I even meet them. I promise that I'll give him a chance."

"Thank you. Now, you better go. It's eight o'clock now and you've still got a ten minute walk to the restaurant."

Leaning to kiss Kate on the cheek, I stood and reached for my purse. The moment I reached the front door of my apartment, I heard my phone ding from inside my bag. Unzipping the bag, I retrieved my phone and looked down at the photo message in horror.

"And…I'm out."

Dropping my bag, I kicked off my shoes, hung up my jacket, and began to undress as I tossed my phone onto the couch with my sister and made my way to the bathroom to draw up a nice hot bath.

"What's wrong?"

Unable to form a proper sentence in response, I simply said, "Just look."

Stunned silence was quickly followed by uncontrollable laughter as Kate read the message and then looked at the photo that would be forever engrained in my mind.

"Hurry up, babe. The bread basket is getting cold. Here's a taste of what you can have for dessert."

Ignoring her cackles, I turned on the hot water all the way. I generously poured bubble bath into the tub and all but dove into the water. When I looked up, Kate stood in the doorway, still laughing hysterically.

"I mean…you gotta give him some credit. Most men lacking in

that way wouldn't feel confident enough to send you a dick pick. Do you want me to text him back for you?"

I rested my forehead against my palm as I shook my head.

"No. There are so many things wrong with that message. It doesn't even deserve a response. First of all, I don't know this man. I don't know where the hell he gets off calling me, 'babe.' Second of all…" The shockingly tiny appendage flashed through my mind and I started to laugh as well. "Second of all…ew. Just block his number for me."

Giggling, Kate turned and left as I disappeared beneath the bubbles.

$\mathcal{I}$ stayed in the tub until I was thoroughly warmed and wrinkled, and I saw Mr. Crinkles paw swipe underneath the closed bathroom door as he tried to get inside. The solid black cat was my sister's baby and the reason she'd not escaped the fire that had destroyed her home unmarred. Not that I could blame her. The cat was ornery, lovable, and incredibly cuddly. After the past six months of having him live under my roof, I was completely in love with him. I would've done exactly as my sister had done if the situation had been reversed.

"Hang on just a second, mister. I'll let you in."

Slipping on my robe and slippers, I opened the bathroom door to allow the cat to slink inside. He immediately dragged his body against my leg before flopping over onto his side between my legs as he purred and begged for me to touch him.

My sister wasn't the only one who lost something in the fire that had pulled me away from my once-in-a-lifetime trip to Scotland so many months ago. Mr. Crinkles—injured by the same beam that had fallen on my sister's right arm—had lost his eye. While it must have been an adjustment for the cat, I quite liked the way he looked with just the one eye—it gave him character and added a little bit of edge to his otherwise friendly disposition.

"Hey, Laurel, if you're out of the tub, come here for a second. I want to show you something."

"You heard her. We've been summoned."

Mr. Crinkles meowed as I lifted him from the floor and carried him into the living room where Kate sat with her eyes glued to the television screen.

"Have you heard of this castle before? Maybe it will provide you some inspiration for your next book."

My next book, which was months past due, didn't exist. I'd been unable to write anything in over a year. I seriously doubted that some television documentary would give me the inspiration I needed to dive back in. Inspiration was the reason I'd left for Scotland, with Marcus in tow as my sidekick, in the first place. I needed an idea, needed to see the sights and the people in the flesh to know which direction my new stories needed to go. I'd almost found it in Scotland, thanks to a mysterious book and an even more mysterious message inside, but just as I'd been about to go in search of answers to the questions the book had posed, we received word of the fire back home, and my trip had come to an immediate end.

"I don't know. What castle is it?"

Lifting her legs, I scooted underneath them as I snuggled into the couch next to her.

"The Castle of Eight Lairds is what it is known as now. I'm sure at one time it had another name, but the documentary hasn't mentioned what it was. Just watch. There's a really fascinating legend behind it."

Something about the name of the castle sounded familiar, but I couldn't recall why. As the commercial ended and the program resumed, I turned my attention to the screen and listened in.

Kate was right. It certainly was an interesting legend, and one, surprisingly, I'd never heard before. If anything was capable of stirring my imagination enough to make me write again, it was this. For the first time in many, many months, an idea began to bud in my mind.

An isle off the mainland of Scotland—much like the name of its castle—was known as The Isle of Eight Lairds, and the story surrounding its legend went back over four hundred years.

The legend went that eight druids must always pledge their magic to the territory and its castle to prevent a hidden darkness from re-emerging and destroying the people of the village. Each generation of eight must pick a new eight to follow them, for if ever one of the eight passes and they are left with just seven, the evil within the castle will rise again and destroy the isle until it is but a blip in Scotland's memory.

The story, as depicted by below-average actors and the narrator's deep baritone voice, weaved a tale of heartbreak, magic, and lore. Of ghosts and banshees and witches. The general consensus now was that little of the legend was true, but I couldn't help but think of the parallels between this story and the one I'd discovered inside Conall Castle so many months ago—of Morna's strange tale of magic and love, and her insistence from the notes inside that all of it was true.

I'd felt the magic throughout Scotland every day I'd been there. I couldn't so easily dismiss the stories, for all stories have some basis in truth. I desperately wanted to know just how much of it was real.

Just as the documentary ended, there was a crash to our left and we both turned to see Mr. Crinkles causing a ruckus on the shelf of one of my bookcases. As I watched one of the books drop to the floor, I realized why the name of the castle had sounded so familiar. Just two weeks earlier, I'd found a book in the middle of the street just a few blocks from my apartment—it was a book about The Castle of Eight Lairds. I'd yet to open it. At the time, the only thing that had been on my mind was how I couldn't bear to see any book left abandoned in the street, so I brought it home. Now, I couldn't wait to look inside.

"Kate, that book that your cat just shoved onto the floor is the one I found the other day. I didn't make the connection until now, but look at what it's called."

Standing, I moved across the room to grab the book. After glancing at the title, I extended it toward Kate's remaining hand.

With eyes wide, she stared down at the cover as her jaw slowly opened in surprise.

"Wow, what are the chances of that? This is a sign, Laurel. This castle is what you're supposed to write about."

My sister was a bit of a wanna-be mystic. She ate up horoscopes, signs, and all things whimsical like candy. But in this instance, I couldn't deny that the coincidence did indeed feel like a sign.

"Maybe so. It definitely has sparked more ideas than I've had in a very long time."

My sister was no longer listening. She'd flipped the book open to a double-spread portrait towards the middle of the book and was staring at the image intensely.

"Laurel, look at this. This guy looks just like Marcus. I mean, just like him."

Leaning over her shoulder, I looked down to see what she was talking about.

Across the page was a group portrait of eight men. Sure enough, the man on the far right end did bear a startling resemblance to my best friend.

Kate twisted to look up at me.

"You should call him, Laurel."

"What for? To tell him that I found a portrait of someone who looks like him? He wouldn't care."

Kate reached up and grabbed my arm to pull me around to the sofa.

"No, of course not for that. It's a strange coincidence—another sign that is perhaps telling you that you need to reach out to him—but I hardly see why Marcus needs to know. You need to call him for you. He's been calling every two weeks for months now. I don't know what happened between the two of you since you've refused to tell me, but I know Marcus, and it couldn't have been anything bad enough to warrant you cutting him out of your life. He's too important to you. You haven't been yourself since the fire. You mope around here pretending to tend to me, which we both know you refuse to do."

She winked at me, and I knew she meant to reassure me that she wasn't angry with how stern I'd been with her. During the first two months following the fire, our mother had stayed in Boston to help me care for Kate. It had been an unmitigated disaster. Heartbroken for her daughter, Mom had doted on Kate in a fashion that only furthered her new difficulties. She would do anything and everything for her. It did nothing but slow her recovery. Eventually, fed up and eager to have my house under my control again, I sent Mom back home to Florida. Kate healed more in the three weeks following our mother's departure than she had in the two months prior, simply because I wasn't as sympathetic. Even when she cried, even when she begged me to do simple tasks that were easy for me to take for granted but were now incredibly difficult for her, I made her do it herself. Each new victory increased her confidence and slowly, she healed.

Seeing how much Kate had improved was the only thing that helped mother forgive me for how I'd treated her.

"Don't get me wrong. I'm glad you've been such a hard ass. I'm just saying, you always pretend that I need you, but you don't really do anything for me when you're here anyway. It's an excuse. I'm tired of being your excuse. It's time for you to get your life back. You need your best friend. You need to start writing again. You're not the one who lost everything in a fire, Laurel, yet you walk around here like you are. Whatever you need to do to get back to the life you had before I moved in here with you, you need to do it."

Someone's words had never had such a profound effect on me. I reeled back on the sofa as if she'd slapped me. She was right, but I didn't know how to begin. Everything felt so completely off course.

"I don't know how, Kate. I don't know what to do. I'm not blaming you. I don't ever want you to think that, but before the fire, I felt like things were just beginning for me, like I was on the verge of some big shift in my life. Then just like that, with one phone call, everything stopped. I floundered, and then I got comfortable in the floundering. Now, I can't see how to pull myself out of it."

Kate leaned forward to pull me into a hug.

"I know you don't blame me, but I've upended your life all the same. And don't worry about what you need to do. Signs always come in threes. You've another one due any time. Just watch for it. You'll know what to do."

Squeezing her tight, I laughed at her confidence.

"Is this what you intend to do for your next career? Are you going to start predicting people's futures?"

Gently pushing me away, Kate stood and reached for Mr. Crinkles.

"It's not fortune telling, Laurel. It's common knowledge. As a writer, I'd think you would know that. Anything important almost always comes in threes."

I smiled at her as she made her way to her bedroom. It took all of three minutes for me to fall asleep on the sofa.

A loud banging on the front door woke me up from a dead sleep at three a.m.

CHAPTER 2

*A*llen Castle—Scotland—1651

*T*he lass was persistent. It was the tenth letter he'd received from her in as many months. He'd yet to open a single one. He knew what he would find—a series of blurred letters to taunt him. Simply more proof that he was losing his sight. And even if he could make out Sydney's words to him, what would he say in return? There was so much he couldn't tell her. Until his land was securely deeded to another, he couldn't tell her the truth of where he lived, or what he did, or even truly, who he was. Until he returned home to the rest of The Eight, he couldn't know if the damage to his eyes was permanent. Even if it was, Sydney was the last person he would want to know. She was one of the few who knew his heart. If he truly lost his vision, he wanted her to remember him as he was before.

As much as it pained him, he would have to let his friendship with her die.

"Thank ye, Madge. Please take this to my bedchamber and leave it with the others."

The old woman nodded but leaned in to quietly whisper in his ear.

"Aye, o'course, sir. If ye'd like to have someone read it to ye, I can have my son come to ye when ye retire this evening. I could assure his discretion."

Raudrich reached out and grabbed her arm as she stepped away to leave him.

"Ye do know that I can read, doona ye, Madge?"

Her voice still low, she answered him.

"Aye sir, but ye canna see the words, can ye?"

His heart sank at Madge's observation. His position as laird was already precarious enough.

"Do others know?"

"I doona believe so. Not many spend as much time with ye as I do. Though ye willna be able to hide it forever.

"Thank ye, Madge. Just leave the letter with the others."

He waited until she was gone from his view before standing from his seat. Music surrounded him as his clansmen danced and drank with merriment. He wished he could enjoy the evening with them, but a strong sense of foreboding made him uneasy. Two tragedies in the span of two months. First, the unexpected death of the man set to replace him as laird, followed shortly by the sudden and swiftly progressing loss of his eyesight. A third tragedy couldn't be far behind—they always came in threes.

He could still see at a distance, though the edges of things were slightly blurred. He hoped it would hold steady until he could find another man to replace him. He'd been away from the eight for far too long, and having his powers stretched over such a great distance and for so long was costing him his vision. Never before had one of the eight stayed away from their magic for so long. Even those who had left for a short while had suffered much, and he'd been away for two and a half years.

He could just make out Silva standing at the end of the hall, hiding under a castle archway as she waved him toward her.

He waited until he neared her to speak. "What is it?"

"A messenger arrived from yer home, Raudrich."

Panic set in at Silva's words. Everything seemed to be falling apart so quickly. She hurried to reassure him by placing a hand on his arm.

"Doona worry. 'Twas I who greeted him. No one else saw the rider arrive or leave. Ye needn't worry."

Silva, the widow of the man set to replace him tonight, knew nothing of the truth about him, but she knew him well enough to see that something was wrong. Otherwise, she wouldn't have hurried to calm his nerves.

There were few among his clansmen that he trusted fully, but he would have to trust Silva with the truth this night. This was a letter he couldn't put off opening.

"Will ye come with me to my bedchamber, Silva? I need ye to read the letter out loud to me, and it must be read in private."

He didn't need to see her face clearly to know that her expression was confused, but she said nothing as he turned to make sure that she followed along behind him.

The moment they were safely inside his room, she spoke.

"Why do ye need me to read this? Surely, there is no need for me to know what is inside."

"I canna see it. A fortnight after yer husband passed, my vision began to decline. Each day it grows a little worse."

Silva's voice was filled with concern.

"What would cause this? Have ye seen the healer about it? Mayhap there is something she can do to help."

"No. I know the cause well enough. All that I doona know is whether or not the vision is restorable. Please read the letter."

He moved to sit as Silva opened the letter. He knew what would be inside.

The third tragedy. He knew there was no other reason for someone from The Land of Eight Lairds to ride here. They all knew how dangerous such a message would be for him.

As Silva began to read, his worst suspicions were confirmed.

Timothy, the oldest of The Eight had lost his long battle with illness. The Eight were now seven, and it was more important than ever that he make preparations to leave Allen territory for good.

Once Silva finished reading the letter, she moved to bend in front of him, gathering his hands in hers.

"Who is this man that ye've lost? Who is so urgently calling ye away from here?"

An unprecedented idea came to mind as he looked at Silva. There was only one thing he could do. With one of The Eight now dead, he couldn't remain here another day.

He took his time explaining everything to her, sparing her no truth.

"When my brother passed, this land became mine, but it is not mine by right. Since the age of thirteen, my loyalty has been pledged to another clan, which, as ye know, voids me of my inheritance. There is a land verra far from here that requires the magic of eight druids to keep the evil that resides within it at bay. Like my grandfather before me, I possess magic. I am one of The Eight. The man that passed was one of The Eight, as well. With The Eight now broken, the evil back at home will begin to look for a way to rise. It is imperative that I return home so we can search for a worthy man to replace Timothy.

"I came here after my brother's death to see the village settled, to make certain that I found a just man to take my brother's stead as laird. It has always been my intention to return to the isle that is now my home. No one else in the clan can ever know of this. If they do, they willna accept the decision I know is right.

"And what decision is that?"

"I must leave here tonight, but first we must find a witness. I shall deed all of my land to ye, Silva. Ye shall be the first female laird of Allen territory."

CHAPTER 3

resent Day

stumbled over to the front door as I called out to my sister to tell her to stay in her room until I found out who was at the door. She replied with a snore. She could sleep through just about anything—even a fire.

"Who's there? Don't you know what time it is?" I stood an arm's length away from the door handle as I called out.

"It's me. Open up." The moment I heard Marcus' voice on the other side, I went limp with relief. Hands shaking, I unlocked the door and threw it open as I stepped aside to let him enter.

"What the hell is wrong with you? You should've called first. You scared me to death banging on the door like that.

He looked around the room with undisguised disgust. He'd not been inside my apartment since Kate moved in. Since then, my aptitude for tidiness, much like my aptitude for just about everything, had slipped significantly.

"You wouldn't have answered if I called. I've been trying to get ahold of you for months."

He moved to shuffle through the pile of mail on my entry table. I quickly moved to block him as I threw my hands down over the stack and glared up at him.

"You can't just go through my mail. What are you doing here?"

"Are you not paying your bills now? Have you turned on a vacuum cleaner in the last three weeks? It smells in here, Laurel."

I was most certainly paying my bills. It was just any other business that I allowed to slip through the cracks.

"It's the cat." I wasn't altogether sure that was true. Kate was a stickler for making certain that Mr. Crinkles' litter box stayed immaculate, but at least the cat was an easy scapegoat. He couldn't argue with me. "And not a single thing on that table is a bill. Of course, I'm paying my bills. I'll ask you one more time, Marcus, what are you doing here?"

"This has gone on long enough, Laurel. I messed up. I know that. I've known it since the words slipped out of my mouth. You're not crazy. I never should have said that you were. I've been trying to apologize to you for months now, but you wouldn't hear it, which frankly, isn't fair. We've been friends for twenty-five years. I should be allowed one mess up. I've certainly forgiven you your fair share of stupidity."

I hardly knew what to say to him. I was still so angry with him, but as he stood before me now, I couldn't recall exactly why. What he'd said had wounded my feelings to be sure, but was it really all that cruel? From his perspective, he believed he was helping me. Perhaps, he was. Was it really myself I was angry at?

"I…" I said the one thing I felt most strongly as I stared back at him. "I've missed you."

I expected him to hug me or at least soften a little at my confession. He did no such thing.

"Have you? Well, I can't really say the same. The longer this has gone on, the angrier I've become at you for pushing me away. But guess what, we are about to fix that. We're going back to Scotland—back to the place where all this fell apart. And we aren't leaving the country until two things happen."

He paused and lifted one finger, followed quickly by a second as he continued.

"One, everything is fixed between us. And two, we know once and for all whether you're mad for believing that old woman's story and her letter to you."

Marcus was the last person I wanted to go looking for Morna's inn with. He didn't for a moment believe that it was there.

"You don't have to do that, Marcus. We don't need to go to Scotland to heal things between us. I forgive you, and I'm sorry for acting like such a child. I think I was angry with myself for hoping, angry for believing that something impossible just might be possible. When you confronted me that day, you made me kill a dream, and it made me resent myself for being so foolish."

He did hug me then—a big, bear of a hug that draped me in more comfort than I'd felt in months. I collapsed into him and began to cry.

"Oh, Laurel." He held me tightly and kissed the top of my head. "I'm a shit friend. Even if I did believe you were mad, I should've just supported you. I've done many things I know you thought were crazy, but you never let me know that. I'm so sorry."

It shouldn't have been the thing I noticed in his apology, but one thing stood out amongst all the rest.

"You just said that you *did* believe I was mad. As if you don't anymore."

He pulled away, but kept both hands on my arms as he held me away from him.

19

"About that…something very strange happened last week that may have changed my mind."

I raised my brows and turned my head like a confused puppy dog.

"Oh, yeah? What's that?"

"I received a letter last week. There was no address, but the country of origin was Scotland, and it was signed by someone named Morna.

A chill swept over my entire body. I didn't believe I'd ever been so surprised in my entire life.

"Morna was the name of the woman who wrote the book I found in Conall Castle."

Marcus nodded.

"I know. The entire letter was just her giving me a thorough lashing for encouraging you to cancel your plans to return to Scotland. How could she possibly know that I'd done that? How could she even know who we are?"

I stared back at Marcus, saying nothing until he broke the silence.

"What are you thinking, Laurel?"

"I shut my mind to the possibility of any of this being real months ago. Now, I don't know what to think. Why did she wait so long to reach out? If she has the ability to know so much about both of us, why not contact me when I was searching for her? And why would she send you a letter? Why not just reach out to me directly?"

Marcus shook his head. He looked as confused as I felt.

"I don't know. But my own curiosity is now piqued enough that I know I won't be able to get anything done until we both find out. I've booked us both on a flight that leaves tomorrow afternoon. If the inn really does exist, we'll find it."

Perhaps, my sister was right and signs really did come in threes.

I couldn't see Marcus' sudden arrival here any other way.

CHAPTER 4

"*W*ell, this is a pleasant surprise."

Dreary-eyed and still a bit wobbly from sleep, Kate entered the kitchen where Marcus and I sat at the table, a road map of Scotland spread across the top. It was just past nine in the morning. We'd spent the rest of the night catching up while he helped me pack.

Marcus stood the moment he saw Kate and moved to wrap his arms around her just as he'd done me the night before. He really did give the very best hugs.

"You look wonderful, Kate. I'm glad to see you getting on so well."

She smiled, but the smile didn't quite reach her eyes. She always tried so hard to stay positive, but every once in a while she couldn't hide her pain.

"Thank you, Marcus. I'm glad, too. It's been a long few months, but I'm feeling a little more like my old self every day. When did you get here?"

He chuckled lightly and bared his teeth in embarrassment.

"About three a.m. actually. I'm afraid I gave Laurel quite the scare. I think I'll run home and get my own bag ready. I'll let Laurel tell you what's going on."

He bent to give her a quick kiss on the cheek before pointing to me.

"I'll be back to pick you up at two. See you in a few hours."

Kate waited until he was gone to say anything.

"Well, that was some night, wasn't it? I went to bed wondering if you two would ever speak again, and I wake up to find the two of you as chummy as ever. What's going on?"

Setting a cup of coffee down on the table for her, I waited for her to sit down to answer. The moment she was seated, Mr. Crinkles jumped up into the empty chair between us and purred so that I would pet him.

"You know how yesterday you were begging me to get my life back and to leave you be for a while since I don't do anything for you anyway? Well, you're about to get your wish. Marcus and I are going back to Scotland this afternoon."

Kate's face lit up with excitement. "To visit the castle in the documentary? I really do think it could be just the place to get you writing again. Oh, Laurel, this is wonderful."

I'd almost forgotten about the castle, but Kate was right. If I was going to be in Scotland anyway, I should definitely pay it a visit to see if it could spark some writing inspiration.

"Well, that castle isn't actually the main reason for our visit, but I do want to get over to it while I'm there."

Kate's smile fell. "Oh. Then, what are you going there for?"

I'd said nothing to anyone about what had happened to me in Scotland, and Kate had been so overwhelmed with her own recovery after the fire that she'd not noticed the hours I'd spent digging for information. It was hardly the sort of story you could tell someone without coming across as insane, but I could see no way to leave without telling her now.

"Would you like to know what happened between me and Marcus all those months ago?"

She nodded and leaned back to sip her coffee.

"So, we had a fantastic trip, but there was something that happened not long before the fire that I haven't told you about. At one of the castles we visited, I came across this book. You know how I am with books—if there's an interesting one just lying around, I can't really keep myself from picking it up. It was the strangest book I'd ever seen. There was a note inside addressed to whoever found it, and it made the point of telling the reader that the story inside was true. Within the first twenty pages, any rational person would realize that the woman's story couldn't possibly be true. It was filled with witches and magic and love, and most surprisingly, time travel. I didn't put the book down until I finished. And then…at the end, there was another note imploring the reader to come and find the woman who wrote it at the inn where her story ended."

I stopped and looked nervously at my sister. Her expression was entirely unreadable.

She waited a long moment before saying anything. I could see by the way she kept pursing her lips that she was thinking through everything I'd just said.

"Well, did you go and visit with the author?"

"That's the thing. The inn she mentioned was along a road that Marcus and I had passed many times. It wasn't there, but the story implied that maybe the inn wasn't always visible. That when we were meant to find it, we would."

"Was it there?"

"I don't know. I got the phone call from Mom about the fire on our way to see. When I got home, I looked for information about this woman, but all I could find was the historical info about a Morna who died back in the seventeenth century. While that would fit with the woman's story, it couldn't possibly be the same woman who wrote the book."

She nodded in agreement.

"Obviously, but you still have to get in touch with her. It's just all too curious to let sit. I'm sure it's been driving you crazy all these months—wondering what that conversation would've been like had you found her."

"It has. The thing is…" I hesitated. It embarrassed me to even say the words out loud. "I sort of believed her story. I know it's impossible, but it just…it felt so real. I don't know. If you'd read it, perhaps you would be able to say the same thing. Anyway, Marcus knew I believed it, and it worried him. When he saw how much time I was investing trying to get to the bottom of this after we got home, he confronted me. He called me crazy and told me I should drop my plan to return to Scotland to search for the woman once you were well. I think what upset me the most is that I was starting to feel a little crazy myself. I lashed out and pushed him away. I haven't looked into the woman any further. But then Marcus showed up last night with some very interesting news."

Kate leaned forward in her seat as her voice lifted with curiosity.

"Which was?"

"He received a letter from someone named Morna, and she somehow knew that he talked me out of returning to Scotland to look for her."

Kate's eyes opened wide.

"What? Are you serious?"

"Completely. And it must've really gotten to him because he showed up here last night already having booked us on a flight out today. Which brings me to you. I know you can take care of yourself, but that doesn't mean you should have to. Will you be okay here? I'm not sure how long we will be gone. If you want, I can call Mom. You know she'd be here by this evening if you wanted her to."

She reached out her hand and placed it on mine as if to stop me.

"Oh God, no. Don't call her. I'll be fine. I promise. I'll call Maggie and she can come and stay with me a few days. Some time alone will be good for me. I miss my independence. It's time I start practicing doing even more by myself. Just promise me one thing."

I smiled and leaned forward to hug her.

"Anything. What is it?"

"If all this does indeed turn out to be true…if the woman is some centuries old witch who travels through time, just give me a call and let me know before you go hurdling through to the past."

I laughed and pulled back assuming she was joking, but there was no humor in her eyes as I stared back at her.

"You don't actually believe that it could be possible, do you?"

She shrugged. "I haven't any idea, Laurel, but isn't it more fun to live in a world where it just might be? Most of what any of us believe about the world is delusional anyway. We might as well believe in delusions that make us smile. The thought of you getting to travel back and get a glimpse of all those wonderful things you write about makes me smile. So…like I said, if it is real, just promise you'll call me."

It was the most ridiculous promise I'd ever made, but I couldn't deny my little sister anything.

"Okay. I promise to call you before I allow a witch to send me into the past."

She smiled as Mr. Crinkles crawled into her lap.

"Good. I can't wait to get that phone call."

25

CHAPTER 5

 *ver the Atlantic Ocean*

*T*he downside of our last-minute flights—besides the exorbitant price that Marcus paid for them—was that we were unable to sit together for the journey. Sandwiched in the middle section, in a middle seat, it was the longest and most miserable travel experience of my life.

The woman to my right smelled of dust bunnies and cheese, and the man to my left liked to spit when he talked. He really liked talking. He was a native Scot, and I wasn't sure I'd ever seen anyone as excited to get home.

"I tell ye, lass, eight weeks is far too long to be away from yer own bed and yer own coffee maker. America is fine in most respects, but none of ye know how to make a proper cup of coffee, and yer breakfasts are terrible. I doona want cereal in skim milk for breakfast. Or worse, a couple of soggy waffles from the hotel buffet. Give me meat and eggs or nothing at all."

27

I wasn't in an appeasing mood.

"I quite like cereal with skim milk."

The man, who'd yet to introduce himself, threw up both hands to cover his heart, accidentally elbowing me in the side of my arm hard enough to make me wince.

"Ach, doona wound me so. I thought ye were a lass with better taste."

"Nope. I'm afraid I have very bad taste indeed. Now, if you'll excuse me, I think I better try to get some sleep. I've got quite a long car drive once we land."

It was the absolute wrong thing to say. It gave him the perfect opening to question me.

"Oh, is that so? Whereabouts are ye headed? I know Scotland like the back of my hand. I could tell ye some bonny places to stop along the way."

I could hardly say anything to him about the inn, so I decided to stick to the closest thing to it.

"Conall Castle, actually. I've always wanted to see it."

This man didn't need to know that I'd visited before.

"Ach, aye, 'tis a lovely castle. There is actually not much to stop and see along yer way there, though the drive is quite beautiful. Where else in Scotland are ye planning to go?"

"The Isle of Eight Lairds."

"Best be careful over there, lass. 'Tis cursed land. Only a few still reside there."

I'd heard this much from the documentary I'd watched with Kate, but I was fairly certain the castle was still open to visitors, and there was a ferry that went out to the isle twice a day.

"I don't believe in curses. Besides, wasn't the original curse from the legend broken at some point? It must have been for the land to have been ruled by one laird at a time rather than eight for the last four hundred years."

The stranger clucked his tongue disapprovingly at me.

"I know nothing of the legend, lass. I only know what I've heard all my life. My own grandfather wouldna step foot on the isle, and there are many in Scotland who feel just as he did. 'Tis mainly foolish tourists like yerself that do."

"You do know that your insistence that this place is cursed has just increased my desire to go there tenfold?"

He shook his head.

"As I said lass...foolish tourists."

---

*M*arcus was several rows in front of me, so by the time I deplaned, he was waiting for me just outside the gate. He looked rested and annoyingly fresh.

"Were you on an entirely different flight than I was? You look great."

He winked and reached for my bag.

"Well, thanks. I'll take it. Rough night, huh?"

"You could say that. I hope you're willing to drive because I'm completely useless. I plan on being asleep five minutes after we pull away from the car rental."

"That's absolutely fine. It's not as if you haven't seen the landscape before. Do you need to stop in at the restroom before we head out?"

His question sounded much more like a suggestion, and by the look in his eye, I could tell that I was right.

"Do I have something on me?"

"No. I just thought..." he squirmed, as if he wasn't quite sure how to say what he wanted to. "I just thought you might want to splash some water on your face, freshen up a little bit. If the inn is there, I assume we will stop before we find a place to stay for the night."

"If it's really an inn, I assume we'll stay there."

He nodded. "Precisely. I know you. I doubt you want to show up looking so tired."

From most people, such a statement would've pissed me off, but I was close enough to Marcus to not take offense to him very politely telling me I looked like crap. I was tired. Of course, I looked that way.

"Okay. You're right. I'll be right back."

I took my time in front of the mirror as I applied a bit of makeup and brushed my hair.

It was always a bit of a strange experience for me to see myself in makeup. In truth, if I was really honest with myself, it was equally strange for me to see myself in real clothes. As a writer, most of my days were spent makeup free, and yoga pants were my work uniform of choice.

Satisfied that I wouldn't frighten anyone, I returned to Marcus and we made our way towards baggage claim.

It took less time than either of us expected for our bags to arrive on the conveyor belt, and as he lugged them along behind us and we made our way out of the airport towards the rental car area, I noticed an old man waving at me from the corner of my eye.

Unthinkingly, I waved back. It was then that I noticed the sign he was holding. Both of our names were written on the small piece of cardboard.

Slapping Marcus' arm a little harder than necessary, I gripped at his arm in my confusion.

"He couldn't possibly mean us, could he?"

I watched Marcus' face as he squinted to make out the names.

"Of course not. No one knew we were coming. It's just...it's just a coincidence." He didn't sound all that convinced. Let's go."

Just as we turned to walk away from him, the old man called out to us.

"Oy, ye two. Get yerselves over here before I freeze to death."

I stopped and turned toward the voice and pointed at the center of my chest in confusion.

"Do ye mean us?"

The man nodded and waved us toward him with his free hand.

"Aye, o'course I do. Laurel is not that common of a name, is it? Get over here so I might introduce myself. Ye willna be needing a car."

Baffled beyond comprehension, Marcus and I both looked at each other for a moment then obediently walked over to the stranger. Placing the sign between his knobby legs, he extended his right hand.

"I'm Jerry, Morna's husband. She dinna wanna risk either of ye not making it to our home this time, so she sent me to fetch ye. Come on now. We best get on. She's not a woman known for her patience."

I took his hand and gripped at Marcus with my left hand to keep myself steady. It wasn't possible that this man was the same one from the story I'd read, but his description matched that of the Jerry in Morna's story exactly.

Realizing that I was shaking his hand for an awkwardly long time, I quickly pulled it away.

"Pick yer chin up, lass. This is only the first of many surprising things ye will learn this day."

I had absolutely no doubt about that.

CHAPTER 6

An Unnamed Village in Scotland—1651

He couldn't make the rest of the journey home alone. His horse knew the path well, but not well enough to lead him home unguided, and he couldn't see well enough to distinguish the paths in front of him. He would stop for the night and spend some time in the local alehouse. In any village, there were people looking for work. Anyone willing to guide him for the rest of the journey would be well paid.

The tavern was boisterous and filled to capacity with both locals and travelers. It took some time for him to get the bar keep's attention once he made his way to the counter.

"Excuse me, sir. Might I ask ye a question?"

Even with bleary eyes, Raudrich could see how weathered the man was. A ragged scar sliced down one side of his face, and the man kept his hair long and disheveled. He was one of the broadest men he'd ever seen.

"Are ye a paying customer? If ye have no intention of drinking or eating here, I'll not be answering anything."

Pulling the small bag from his kilt, he plopped three coins down in front of the man.

"I'll be doing both."

Quickly sliding the coins toward him, the barkeep twisted and hollered to someone in the back room to bring him some food.

"Then I'm pleased to make yer acquaintance. Name's Pinkie. What can I do for ye?"

Raudrich had never heard such a strange name before. He couldn't help but ask.

"Is that yer real name?"

"O'course it isna my real name, but 'tis the name I gave ye."

Raudrich liked the man already. He was as rough around the edges as many of the other eight.

"Verra well." He extended his hand. "I'm Raudrich, and I'm in need of a hired hand to lead me home. Do ye know of anyone in the village who is trustworthy, knows the country well, and is in need of work?"

"Ye need a guide to take ye home? Are ye lost? Do ye not know the way yerself?"

Pinkie's questions were valid. He only wished he didn't have to answer them. He was weakened in his current state. It wasn't something that he believed he would ever grow accustomed to.

"I'm not lost. I know the way verra well. 'Tis only that my eyes are failing me. They grow worse each day. I canna see the path to lead my horse."

The brief silence before the man's response was filled with the one thing he loathed most in the world—pity. It was what he dreaded most about losing his sight—knowing that others would pity him.

"I see. And where is yer home?"

"The Isle of Eight Lairds."

The man's reaction was exactly as expected.

"'Tis a far journey. Ye shall have to pay someone much for them to agree to be away from their own home so long."

"Aye, I know. I would prefer to hire someone without family. If it is someone without work, they can set their own wage. If ye have someone in mind who already has work, I will double whatever they make now for as long as the journey takes."

The man who must've been in the back taking Pinkie's orders suddenly slipped in next to him and placed a steaming plate of food down on the counter. He looked up to thank him.

"Thank ye, sir. It smells delicious."

Pinkie leaned in close and whispered in his ear as he bent down to eat.

"Ye best eat quickly. Old man Stuart will have ye thrown out on yer arse just as quick as ye can say gypsie the moment I tell him that ye've just hired me away from him. I'll meet ye outside just as soon as I tell him the news."

Raudrich turned to look at the man and spoke below his breath as he watched Stuart return to the kitchen out of the corner of his eye.

"Pinkie, I dinna mean ye. I was asking if ye knew of someone who would be good for the job."

His new friend laughed and clasped him on the shoulders.

"Too bad. 'Tis me that ye've got. Ye just said ye would be doubling my wages, and I'll get to leave this hellhole for the foreseeable future. I'd sooner pull out my one good tooth before I let ye hire someone else."

"Verra well. Eating quickly shouldna be a problem. I'm starving. I'll see ye outside shortly."

At least he knew the remainder of his journey home wouldn't be a dull one.

CHAPTER 7

M *orna's Inn—Present Day*

W riters live in stories. We spend most of our days vividly imagining the worlds we are creating when we write. It's sometimes even worse when we read. With our imaginations already overactive and without the pressure of having to create the world ourselves, we read and are truly taken away to the world the writer has created for us. Pulling up in front of the inn in the same car as a man I'd read so very much about felt like stepping right into a storybook.

It looked exactly as I imagined it would. With the unbelievable act of Jerry awaiting us in the airport, I felt the old hope and dreaming rise up inside me again. That little voice that whispered *"what if"* so many months ago when I'd read Morna's story in one of the bedrooms of Conall Castle crept back into my mind.

Marcus appeared bug-eyed with shock. Even with the letter, he'd been certain someone was playing tricks on us. He never believed for a moment that the inn would actually be here. The fact that it was had him more than a little rattled.

As soon as Jerry parked the car out front and exited the vehicle, I turned to him.

"Are you okay? You look like you might be ill."

"This inn was not here before. You know that, right?"

I nodded. "Yes. I do know that."

"Then how is it here now? How do you explain this?"

"I don't know. I can't explain any of it any more than you can." I reached out to squeeze his hand gently. "I don't mean to sound harsh, but I have a feeling you better strap in. Everything so far is exactly how she described it. If this trend continues, we're in for a bunch more unexplainable things."

Knuckles rapped against the window, and I twisted to see Jerry smiling, his face all but plastered against the glass.

"Just what are the two of ye doing? I told ye that my wife is not a patient woman. Leave yer bags and come on inside. We can get those in a bit."

I didn't wait for Marcus to exit the car. I was now too excited to worry too much about his psychological wellbeing. I wanted to see the inside of Morna's home. Even more than that, I wanted to see Morna, worse than just about anything I'd ever wanted in my whole life.

She stood just inside the doorway, her graying hair framing a face that was still just as beautiful as I'd known it would be. Looking at her, there was no doubt in my mind that she was the same Morna from the story. The only question was how much of her novel was true.

"Laurel, lass, it certainly has taken ye long enough to get here, though o'course I understand why. 'Tis terrible what happened to yer sister, though I can promise ye it will all work out just fine for her in the end. Come here and give me a hug."

Of course she knew about Kate. I doubted there was anything I could tell her about myself that would surprise her.

"I…" I faltered as I walked toward her with open arms. "It's lovely to finally meet you. I have to tell you, I feel as if I know you after reading your book."

"Why, surely ye hear the same thing from yer own readers often, do ye not?"

I laughed as her arms wrapped around me. She was significantly shorter than me, and I had to crouch to bring myself down to her level.

"Not really. Though, my stories aren't about me. They're about the characters that choose to tell their own stories through me."

"Ah. Well, I suppose 'tis true."

Releasing me, she grabbed my hand and led me to a cozy living room just off the main entry.

"Come, dear. I know ye must have lots of questions for me."

"You have no idea."

She turned to wink as she laughed.

"Oh, I bet I do. Though, let's wait until yer friend recovers from his shock and comes to join us. 'Twill be easiest to explain everything to the both of ye once."

As if summoned, Marcus appeared in the doorway. I took a seat on the couch as Morna stood to greet him. After simple niceties were exchanged, Marcus joined me. After a short moment of awkward silence, Morna spoke.

"All right ye two, should I go first, or would ye like to?"

I had a list of questions I'd been waiting to ask her for months. I raised my hand as if I were in school.

"I'll go."

She nodded and lifted her palm from her lap to tell me to begin.

"How much of the story was true? Obviously, the love story

was, but the rest of it—the time travel, the magic—it can't be real, right?"

She seemed surprised by my question.

"I have to say, lass, 'tis not what I expected ye to ask me. If it wasna true, how could ye be here right now? How could I have written to Marcus? How could I have known ye were returning to Scotland? If the magic wasna real, why would I have needed to see ye?"

I smiled and shook my head as I shrugged.

"I don't have the slightest idea on any of it. For argument's sake, let's say everything in your story was true—that you are a witch born centuries before now—that still doesn't explain why you needed to see me at all. You don't know me. Why would you want me, of all people, to read your story?"

"I doona choose who I'm meant to help, lass. The names and faces come to me at all times of day, and yers came through clear as a bell."

I didn't feel as if I was in need of any help whatsoever.

"And just how are you meant to help me? Do you plan on sending me into the past?"

She smiled and nodded excitedly.

"Aye, precisely."

Marcus spoke up for the first time since sitting.

"Not that I believe any of this, but why? Why would Laurel need to go into the past?"

A small piece of Morna's story entered my mind, and a nagging nervousness lodged itself in my stomach as I whispered the answer under my breath.

"She's a matchmaker."

Jerry spoke up from across the room.

"What's that, love? I canna hear as well as I once could."

I straightened in my seat as I looked directly into Morna's eyes.

"You're a matchmaker, right? If that's what you're trying to do with me, let me just bid you good day now. I'm so not even remotely interested."

Marcus chuckled, and I had to press my palms into my legs to keep from shoving him off the couch.

"Why not? Lord knows you need a man in your life, Laurel. You might as well be a nun as empty as your love life is."

Morna laughed and Jerry quickly joined in. I glared back at all of them.

"Doona worry, lass. 'Tis true that I've been known to make a few matches now and again, but 'tis not how I intend to help ye."

I relaxed noticeably in my seat.

"Okay. Well, then why exactly do I need your help?"

She raised her brows as if I should already know the answer.

"How long has it been since ye've written?"

I knew the answer by heart.

"Thirteen months and sixteen days."

"That is how I shall help ye, lass. I will send ye back for inspiration. So that ye may find the exact story ye were meant to tell."

That appealed to me much more than I wanted her to know.

"And in what century does my inspiration lie and where in Scotland?"

"The year 1651 on The Isle of Eight Lairds."

A familiar chill swept over me—the same I'd felt when glancing at the book that Mr. Crinkles pushed from my shelf.

"The book?"

"Aye, the book and the documentary, o'course. I intended for ye to see them both." In response to my open mouth, she chuckled and continued. "Do ye really believe that coincidences are ever truly that? Let me assure ye, 'tis not the way this world works. People are so unwilling to see the tiny miracles, the tiny pieces of magic, that happen in their lives almost every day. 'Tis a shame really."

I smiled as Kate sprung up in my mind.

"You sound like my sister."

Standing, Morna motioned for us to do the same.

"Yer sister is wiser than most people give her credit for. Now, come. Let's get a bite of food in the both of ye. I've much to explain and prepare ye for. Ye are due in the village on The Isle of Eight Lairds tomorrow at noon."

"We?" Marcus sounded horrified. "I'm not going into the past."

Laughing, Morna placed her hand gently on his back as she guided him out into the hallway.

"Aye, ye are. 'Tis the only way ye will ever truly believe any of this."

"You're right about that, but it still doesn't mean that I want to go."

Morna wasn't interested in arguing with him at all.

"Tough. Ye are going, and that is the end of it. Yer destiny is more tied to the isle than Laurel's."

Before Marcus could ask what she meant, Jerry, who'd walked on ahead of us, hollered after his wife from inside the kitchen.

All I could think of as I followed after them was the portrait inside the book. At the time, I'd simply thought the man resembled Marcus. Was it possible that it actually had been him?

Was Marcus destined to be one of the legendary eight?

CHAPTER 8

"*D*on't tell me that you're becoming a time traveler already?"

It was midnight back home, but Kate sounded completely awake when she answered her phone.

"Actually…I think I just might be."

"What?" Her voice was a high-pitched screech that caused me to hold the phone away from my ear. "Are you serious? I truly had been sort of joking."

"I know you were. I mean, let's be realistic, every logical part of me tells me that come noon tomorrow that when this supposed witch casts her spell, Marcus and I will look around to find ourselves totally unmoved. I know that. And that's totally okay with me. I just made you a promise that I would call should the need arise, and according to Morna, it has."

"How will I know if it is real?"

"Well, I'm quite sure that this woman is harmless, so you needn't be worried about her harming us. If her spell does nothing, I'll call you the moment Marcus and I leave here. If you don't hear from me tomorrow, then I guess you can assume that it worked."

Kate sighed, and the sadness in her breath made me hurt all over.

"What's wrong? Do you need me? If you do, I'll head back home right now, Kate."

"No, nothing's wrong. I'm a little jealous, is all. An adventure like that sounds amazing. Also, you should know. Mom called me this afternoon, and I made the very stupid mistake of telling her where you'd gone. She's booked on the next flight out here tomorrow."

That went a very long way to explaining the sigh.

"Oh, Kate. I'm sorry. Whatever you do, don't let her do everything for you. The last thing you need is to have her coddling delay your progress."

"I know. I won't."

I immediately felt guilty for ordering her around. She wasn't a child. She knew better than I what was best.

"I'm sorry. I just worry about you."

"I know you do. How long will you be gone? You'll be able to come back right?"

"Of course, I will. I could never leave you and Mr. Crinkles. I've become quite attached to that damn cat. Morna says whenever I'm ready to leave all I need to do is place a letter to her in the fireplace, and she will return us to her inn. Sounds simple enough."

"Sounds a little too simple."

Kate's tone was suspicious. I understood why. I'd had the same foreboding feeling when Morna had explained everything to me.

"It does, doesn't it? But, I can hardly argue with her."

"Where are you going?"

When I told her where, she repeated the shriek she'd let out earlier.

"I told you that book was a sign! The documentary too! You know, Laurel, I've never been jealous of you. Not once in our whole lives. I always thought I'd lose my mind if I had a life as isolated as yours, but right now I'm so green with envy I could burst."

"I suppose if Mom starts to drive you too crazy, you could always come. Morna knows who you are, and I'm pretty sure she already likes you. Just have her send you back, too."

The words slipped out unthinkingly, and I regretted them right away. It wasn't right of me to assume that Morna would be willing to do any such thing, and I knew Kate well enough to know that before the fire, it would've been just the sort of thing she would jump on.

"Mmm…if only, big sis. This century has enough difficulties for me now. I imagine several hundred years in the past would be even far less accessible for someone with my challenges. If you can though, if there's any way, please let me know what's going on with you. And promise me you won't stay too long."

"I promise."

The door to the bedroom Morna had placed me in opened and Marcus stepped quietly inside before gently closing the door. He looked frightened. Covering the speaker so Kate couldn't hear, I mouthed to him,

"What's wrong?"

"Laurel, I'm scared. I think we need to get out of here right now."

I held up a hand to stop him and hurriedly bid my sister farewell. The moment I ended the call, I stood up and walked over to him.

"Why? What are you talking about?"

"I was in the bathroom just about to brush my teeth when I heard voices from what I assume is their bedroom. It was coming through the vent. Jerry seemed to be trying to keep his voice low, but with his bad hearing, he speaks more loudly than he realized."

Marcus was shaking he was so worked up.

"Okay, and what did they say?"

"He was scolding Morna, telling her she shouldn't have lied to us, but if we believed her we were daft fools. He said we had a right to know what we were getting ourselves into. That it wasn't right for her send us back without us knowing there was no way to return."

"What?" I dropped to the edge of the bed. He might as well have kicked me straight in the stomach for as ill as I suddenly felt. "Are you certain that's what he said?"

"I'm sure. Laurel, I have a life back home. People I love. A job I love. I don't want to be here. Not for even a minute more."

I nodded in agreement and stood as I began to pace. My bag was still packed.

"Where's your bag?"

"I packed it before I came in here. We need to go. Now."

Reaching for my bag, our biggest obstacle came rushing to the forefront of my mind, and I had to reach for the edge of the bed for support.

"We don't have a car, Marcus"

"I saw Jerry's keys laying on the entranceway table. We're stealing the car. I'd rather end up in a Scottish prison than trapped in another century for the rest of my life. Let's go."

I was inclined to agree with him.

We exited the room as quietly as we could, and Marcus lifted his bag from the top of the staircase before we made our way downstairs.

I could see the keys glistening under the lamp on the table right by the front door. Marcus moved ahead of me to grab them and hurriedly opened the door. As I moved toward it, the handle swung out of his hand and the door slammed shut in my face.

I'd never experienced such overwhelming fear in my life.

We faced the stairway together and stared into Morna's rather surprisingly sympathetic eyes.

"I really am sorry about this. I'd hoped for the journey to be consensual, but I'm afraid I canna allow ye to leave. Neither of ye know just how important 'tis that ye go."

Marcus stepped forward with rage in his eyes, but just as he opened his mouth to speak, the room began to spin. I reached for him, and as I latched onto his arm, everything went black.

CHAPTER 9

The Castle of Eight Lairds—1651

There was hay everywhere. It stuck out the top of my shirt, poked me in the bum, and I suspected it would take me hours to get all of it out of my hair. I was disoriented and I hurt all over. I blinked slowly as I strained to try and focus my vision. Large, beautiful brown eyes stared down at me. As I tried to push myself up and out of the giant mound of hay, the horse to my right neighed happily. If I didn't know any better, I would've said he looked rather amused. I was sure it wasn't every day that strange women fell from the sky and into his hay.

"Marcus?"

He grunted in response. Reaching for the stable door, I pulled myself up and looked over at the other side where Marcus lay balled up on the floor.

"Are you okay?"

He lifted his head to look at me.

"I'm alive."

"Well, get up and get in here with me. If someone comes in, at least we can hide in here. We need to figure out what to do."

Marcus was angry. I could tell from the way the muscles in his jaw were bulging as he ground his teeth.

"My head is splitting, Laurel. What did that damned witch do to us?"

My head hurt, as well, but I had too much on my mind to pay the pain any mind.

"She did exactly what she told us she was going to do. She sent us back in time."

Lifting the latch on the stall, Marcus opened the door and stepped inside with me and the horse.

"We're stuck here, Laurel. I heard what Jerry said to her. He said there was no way for us to get back."

I couldn't allow myself to believe that was true. I knew Morna through the story she'd shared with me. She wasn't evil. She wouldn't upend someone's life so completely without a reason. I would say nothing to Marcus about the book and his portrait inside, but I suspected the reason we were here had everything to do with him. If I had to guess, I assumed I was here for moral support and maybe—as she'd said—to regain some inspiration for my writing.

"I don't believe that. And you can't allow yourself to wallow in that hole, either. She said that we were meant to be here. Maybe there is something we are supposed to do, some role we are meant to play, and when we've completed it, we will be able to return home."

Marcus didn't appear to be convinced.

"And what role is that? We know no one here. We will both stand out like sore thumbs. We have nowhere to stay, no way to earn money. Heck, I don't even know how money works in this time. We will be lucky if we survive a week here."

"I don't know."

As if she'd heard his worries from centuries ahead, there was a loud, sudden thump on the other side of the stall wall where I'd found Marcus. I leaned over to find a pile of folded clothes with a letter on top.

"You've got to be kidding me."

Marcus retrieved the items and ripped open the letter as he leaned against the side of the stall. I reached out to stroke our new equine friend as he read the letter aloud.

Laurel and Marcus,

I am truly sorry for the scare I've given you. While I've been known to surprise others with the travel, never before have I sent someone through when they believed me capable of ill intent. I promise that I mean you no harm. I know you must have many questions. Firstly, put on these clothes straight away. Unless, ye wish to be burned for witchcraft, doona let anyone see you dressed as you are now.

Laurel, you are in the stables of the castle you wish to visit. Had you traveled back tomorrow, I would've placed you on their front steps, but since you made me send you in the middle of the night, I thought it best you hide out until morning. Some of The Eight travel down to the village every third day to check on their tenants and to see to the needs of their people. Tomorrow is just such a day. Best be out of their stables by sunlight lest you wish to be accused of trying to steal their horses.

When you approach the castle, tell whomever greets you that you are here to see Laird Allen. He's familiar with me. He'll know what to do with you.

Marcus, I've never been one to mince words, so I'll not dance around something I'm sure you already know. Things may not be easy for you here. The color of your skin may subject you to unfair prejudice, and I am sorry for it. What I can promise you is that the men within this castle are different. While you are among them, they will protect you and treat you as the equal that you are. When Laurel gains entry to the castle, insist that you would never allow Laurel to enter without an escort. They will expect to know what you are to her, and a friend simply won't do. Say you are adoptive siblings. They should allow you to stay at the castle, as well.

Once there, try to relax and enjoy. Get to know the men. Get to know the castle. It won't take long for the reason I've sent you here to be clear.

I'll be watching. If you ever truly need me, I'll be there.

Much love,

Morna

P.S. If it makes you feel any better, Jerry is very cross with me. He wanted you to know that. He tried to talk me out of all this many, many times.

When Marcus finished reading the letter, he crumpled it up and threw it as hard as he could across the stables.

"This is madness, Laurel. What are we supposed to do until tomorrow?"

I patted my new friend as the horse leaned his large head into my hands. I could see that Marcus was angry, worried, and grappling with how any of this could be real. I was worried for him, too.

"Hey." I walked across the stall and reached for his hands. "Are you okay? I believe what Morna says. I don't think she would allow anything to happen to you. If she says that these men are different, I'm certain they are. And as for what we do, I guess we hang out with this big fellow." I patted the horse as if Marcus didn't already know who I meant. "At least we are safe in here, and it will be far warmer than camping outside."

Marcus' angry expression softened as he pulled one of his hands away from mine to gently cup the side of my face.

"Laurel, as angry as I am with the witch, I'm glad she didn't bullshit me. Of course, things will be trickier for me here. Although, I imagine things will be more difficult for you here, as well. I'll be fine. Anything that is said to me, I doubt it will be anything I haven't heard before. And I agree, if there is any real danger posed to me, surely if Morna has the power to send us here, she has the power to help me out of a bind. I want you to promise me something, Laurel."

"What?"

"When ignorance rears its ugly head—which it's bound to—please keep your mouth shut. I know you mean well, but sometimes you tend to make things worse. I can handle myself, okay?"

I knew he was right. Marcus might as well have been my brother for as protective as I was of him.

"I'll do my best."

He smiled and threw me the dress he'd draped over the side of the stall and closed his eyes tight.

"That's all I ask. Now, let's get changed. The next time I see Morna, I'm going to kill her."

Laughing, I began to undress. Marcus was the gentlest man I knew. "Says the man who called me when a mouse got into his apartment."

"All right. Maybe I won't kill her, but I'm definitely going to give her a piece of my mind."

"I'm sure you will. Now, help me tie this up, and can you please just try and enjoy this a little bit? We've stepped into a world most people have never seen."

It took a few hours of visiting and me making every possible effort to make him laugh, but as the night wore on, Marcus relaxed.

By the time we stopped talking and decided to try and get some sleep, he was as curious about what the next day would bring as I was.

Our excitement was replaced with fear as we were both startled awake at dawn.

CHAPTER 10

The Castle of Eight Lairds

ifted up by my arms in the middle of a deep sleep, I struggled fruitlessly against the hands that gripped at me as I woke.

A giant of a man with curly red hair and a frizzy red beard held me away from him as I found my footing. He smiled widely but shook his head and clucked his tongue before speaking.

"Ye two are the worst thieves I've ever seen. Ye fell asleep in the middle of yer jobs."

"We're not…we're not thieves."

I glanced over to see Marcus who was being held back by a tall but slender man with dark hair that was cropped short and eyes that were a startling blue. His face was grim. He looked remarkably serious.

Marcus said nothing. He still looked half-asleep.

The man in front of me—seemingly deciding that I was no

threat—released his grip on me as he crossed his arms across his chest.

"Oh, really? Then how and why did ye climb our gates in the dead of night, and why are ye asleep in the stall with our finest horse?"

"We were on our way to see Laird," I completely drew a blank on the name Morna mentioned in her letter. "Laird...Laird Aldridge. He's expecting us."

Marcus groaned, and I knew that I'd said the wrong name.

The man in front of me laughed. "Laird Aldridge? There is no such man here."

"I...I mean Laird Albert."

I knew the second I uttered the name that it was wrong, as well. In an attempt to save me, Marcus spoke up for the first time. It was a struggle to refrain from literally facepalming myself on the forehead. I felt like a total idiot.

"Laird Allen. We are here to see Laird Allen."

The man turned to face Marcus.

"And ye say he's expecting ye? Ye think I should believe that when this lassie," he paused and pointed his thumb at me, "doesna even know his name? Do ye know him?"

I tried to recover.

"I do know his name. You just startled me, is all. And we do know him. As I said, he's expecting us."

He swiveled back toward me.

"This shall be fun, lass. Okay, if ye truly do know him, pray tell me what he looks like."

I was an imbecile. I glanced back and forth between the two men and pleaded with Marcus with my eyes for help. He simply shrugged.

"It's been a very long time since I last saw him. I would've been a small child, really. Although, I do remember that he is very tall."

"Just how tall would that be, lass?"

I pursed my lips and attempted to look like I was trying to remember. "I would say just a little bit shorter than you."

For the first time since our exchange began, the man holding Marcus' arms released him and cracked a silent smile.

The red-haired man shook his head and smiled even more widely.

"Ye've managed to make Calder smile. He doesna smile for anyone. I suppose that means that thief or not, we canna kill ye. 'Twould break his heart."

My eyes must have widened with worry for the man hurried to reassure me.

"Doona fash, lass, I only speak in jest. We wouldna ever kill ye. Now, do ye have any idea what ye said that might've made Calder smile so?"

I shook my head. I didn't have any idea.

"Lass, Laird Allen canna be more than a few years older than ye are. I doona believe that he was my height at the age of ten."

"Damnit."

The redhead's eyes widened.

"'Tis unladylike to curse, lass."

"Ha." Marcus seemed to be enjoying the spectacle I was making of myself. His smile was as wide as Calder's. "There's nothing ladylike about Laurel."

The redhead raised his brows at me in question.

"Is that so, lass? Ye look like quite the proper lady."

I shot Marcus a frown. I was low-maintenance to be sure. I didn't fuss with fashionable clothes, and I never paid more than twenty dollars for a tube of mascara, but I'd never considered myself unladylike. Perhaps, I did need to start trying just a little harder. I didn't like the thought of anyone thinking of me as a manly slob.

"I...I am too ladylike." My answer sounded ridiculously childish.

The redhead gave me a sympathetic look. "O'course ye are. Laurel, was it?"

I nodded.

"'Tis a bonny name." He extended his hand to me, and I gladly took it. His grip was firm and his handshake was a little over exuberant, but it made me like him immediately. "I'm Harry."

"It's nice to meet you, Harry." I pointed to Marcus once my hand was free. "This is my brother, Marcus."

As expected, Harry's brows lifted as his trademark smile spread across his face once again. He was looking at the obvious difference in our skin colors and not buying it for a second.

Harry extended his hand toward Marcus and spoke as they shook. "Yer brother? Are ye sure ye dinna mean to say friend or mayhap, lover?"

Marcus spoke and the lie sounded remarkably believable even to me. "Her parents took me in when I was young. I'm her brother in every way that matters."

Understanding spread across Harry's face, and I could see right away that Morna had been truthful. There was no malice in the man's doubt, only curiosity. "Neither of ye are from here, aye? Not that I rightly care, to be sure. 'Tis only that I've never heard such speech in my life. I've already told ye Calder's name. He's a shy one. Ye willna get much out of him. Now." He clasped his palms together and rubbed them back and forth excitedly. "Calder and I are expected in the village shortly. 'Tis time we decide what to do with ye."

"What to do with us? Are you not going to let us speak to Laird Allen."

"Laird Allen isna here. He hasna been in two and a half years. I doona expect he will be here for another fortnight, at least. While I doona believe for a moment that ye know him or that ye even have business with him, I like ye well enough that I'm willing to host ye until he returns. I'm verra curious to see how he responds to ye."

For the first time, Calder spoke up, his tone was filled with warning.

"She's a lassie, Harry. She canna stay in the castle. 'Tis not allowed."

Harry waved a dismissive hand.

"Calder, 'tis a foolish superstition—one we should've tested long ago. She tries to control us through fear. 'Tis likely that much of what she says is untrue. I hardly believe that having one lass inside these walls will cause us trouble."

"Let us at least have them stay in the village, Harry. 'Twill be safer for everyone."

Harry gestured toward the stable doors with a small nod of his head. Together, we all began to move toward the exit.

"Ach, doona be such a worrier, Calder. 'Twill send ye to an early grave. 'Twill lift everyone's spirits to have a lass about—even yers, I reckon."

As Harry pushed the large doors open, we stepped out into the fresh air, and Marcus and I got our first look at The Castle of Eight Lairds. It was even more gothic and intimidating than it appeared in the documentary. Dark, dead vines creeped up the front, and the forest surrounding it dropped off steeply on each side.

Marcus muttered under his breath, "Wow."

Harry clasped Marcus on the shoulder. "'Tis even more impressive in the daytime, aye?"

Marcus nodded as Calder stepped over near Harry. "I doona think this a good idea."

Harry's tone dropped and I noticed that his face—when he wasn't smiling—made him appear very unfriendly.

"I doona care what ye think, Calder. See them settled inside while I ready our horses. Place Marcus in Timothy's old room. Place Laurel in the castle's finest bedchamber."

"But that's Raudrich's room."

Harry nodded. "Precisely. Raudrich has always had a soft place in his heart for the lassies. He willna have the heart to remove her once he arrives, and it will keep the rest of us from being unsettled. He can sleep elsewhere."

Without another word, Harry turned to leave us. Desperate to see the inside of the castle, I all but chased after Calder as he walked inside.

CHAPTER 11

*T*he rest of the day passed rather strangely. After Calder showed us to our individual rooms, he informed us that the other men of the castle were out in the forest working and that the master of the castle—whatever that meant—was already in the village for the day. He told us to make ourselves at home, to explore as we wished, and to be in the dining hall for dinner at sundown.

It was all very strange. While Calder was polite, he did nothing to hide his disapproval of Harry's order. I couldn't blame him.

It was one thing to allow us to stay here until Laird Allen returned. It was another thing entirely to leave us unattended in a massive castle that was undoubtedly filled with all sorts of valuable items.

I loved it. I couldn't remember a time when I'd been more excited about anything. I'd thought touring Scottish castles long after their prime was the peak of excitement. I was wrong. Touring them in this time, as a guest, was something I would be able to live off of for years.

It was unlike any other Scottish castle I'd ever seen. Gothic and exaggerated, each new wing was creepier than the last. And it was blatantly obvious that men lived and ruled here. It lacked anything feminine or fancy. Everything was for function, nothing for fuss.

Marcus and I spent the day familiarizing ourselves with the castle. About an hour before sunset, we each went to our room to freshen up.

I was ready way before Marcus. He was notorious for taking forever to get ready for anything. I waited inside my borrowed room until he came for me.

"You ready?" He called to me through the door just as the sun dipped below the bedchamber's tall window, and I threw the door open with way too much force.

"So ready."

He smiled at me and offered his arm.

"You look good, Laurel. More like yourself. As angry as I am at that witch, I'm pleased that you're enjoying this so much. You needed something to bring you back to life."

*T*he ruckus from the dining hall could be heard as soon as we descended the castle's grand stairway, but the moment Marcus and I stepped into the room, it fell completely silent.

"Hi." It was literally the only thing I could think to say as seven men who were even more impressive in stature than Marcus rose from their seats around the table.

Harry was the first to speak.

"Laurel, lass, ye look even lovelier than ye did this morning. Ye and yer brother come around here so I may introduce ye to everyone."

Nodding, we made our way to the side of the long table where there were two empty seats waiting for us.

He wasted no time in making introductions. I paid special attention as I was determined to do a better job of remembering each of their names than I was usually capable of doing.

"Calder, o'course."

He pointed briefly to the man we'd already met and then moved his finger to the next man around the table.

The man had solid gray hair that fell just below his chin. He had kind but sad green eyes and stubble along his cheeks that was a slightly darker shade of grey. He was easily the oldest man at the table. He was also the shortest. He looked like he hadn't slept in weeks.

"This is Nicol. He is the master of the castle and the man whom we all serve."

Nicol dipped his head in recognition and gave us both a smile that made my heart ache. He looked heartbroken and pained.

"Greetings to ye both. Ye are welcome here as long as ye wish. Any friend of Raudrich's is a friend of mine."

Out of the corner of my eye, I noticed Calder begin to open his mouth, but before he could say anything, Harry elbowed him straight in the ribs and gave him a look that made it clear he'd not told the rest of the men the truth about who we were.

I muttered a quick greeting and a thank you to him before Harry continued his introductions.

The next, a man named Quinn, had brilliantly blonde hair that fell to his waist. His eyes were dark brown. He was striking in the most unusual way.

Next to Quinn sat Ludo. Ludo had the coolest curls I'd ever seen. They framed his face in a way that would make any girl envious, and his honey-colored eyes matched the shade of his hair. I was certain he had no trouble wooing ladies.

At the table's end was Paton. He was easily the youngest. I couldn't imagine that he was much older than twenty. He had jet black hair that he kept pinned at the nape. His brown eyes were kind and soft.

Finally, Harry ended his introductions with the man directly to Marcus' right—Maddock. He had broad shoulders and strong arms —a trait every man around the table shared. Maddock kept his hair cut short, although it was slightly longer on top. His hair was a dirty blonde and he had green-gold eyes. His nose was slightly large, with a knot in the middle which was a sure giveaway that at some point he'd broken it. His cheeks were smattered with freckles. I couldn't explain why, but I felt an immediate kinship with this man. He reminded me of someone I'd known before, but I couldn't recall who.

When all introductions were made, we sat down to enjoy our meal.

"Who did the cooking?"

Ludo answered with pride in his eyes, straight away.

"Tonight, 'twas I, but we share all duties equally. Tomorrow is Quinn's turn so if ye are wise ye will fill yer belly tonight. Quinn is a rubbish cook."

Quinn tried to protest but was quickly silenced by the chorus of voices who chimed in to agree with Ludo.

Once their teasing ended, Ludo spoke up once again.

"We doona have help here at the castle, so we must all do our part. 'Tis why it is time for Raudrich to return home. We've all been doing his share of the work for far too long. He has much to make up for. If ye doona mind me asking, how exactly is it that ye know him?"

I felt the light tap of Harry's foot on top of my own. A slightly more gentle warning than he'd given Calder.

I winked at him to let him know I understood while I scrambled for a believable explanation.

Morna was a Conall and she'd claimed that Raudrich knew of her. Perhaps I could claim relation to them.

"I'm a distant cousin to the laird of Conall territory. As you know, Laird Allen is friends with the Conalls. We met while were both staying at the castle many years ago—when we were children."

Paton chimed in from the table's end.

"And why do ye need to see him now? I'm surprised that ye knew he was here. To the people of this territory, Raudrich has another name. He's had to keep his identity a secret to protect his familial clan."

He might as well have been speaking gibberish. There was so much about this time, about their customs and the rules among clans that I didn't know. I would have to tread carefully.

Marcus didn't allow me the time to formulate an answer. "She's in love with him."

The blood drained from my face as I shrank in my chair in horror.

Every man around the table looked as shocked as I felt.

I could see that Harry was struggling to suppress his laughter. "In love with him, ye say? Promise us that ye will wait to tell him that until we are all around to see it."

Meekly, I tried to respond with something reasonable. "I think that's something best expressed in private."

"Right ye are, lass." Harry stood and the rest of the men followed suit. "I think it best we all retire early. Ye two must be tired after yer journey."

Clearly the rest of them didn't know about our night in their stables. Although, I couldn't disagree with him. I was exhausted and I couldn't wait to sleep on a seventeenth century bed. I had no idea what to expect.

"I can't speak for Marcus, but I am rather tired. Thank you all so much for your hospitality."

"'Tis our pleasure, lass. Mayhap tomorrow I can get ye to help me with something?"

"Of course. I'd be happy to help you all in any way I can."

"Good."

It was evident from the way every man stood around the table unmoving that they were waiting to disband until we made our leave. Glancing at Marcus to make sure he was on the same page, we stood and left the dining hall.

Baring my teeth, I whispered to him through my clenched jaw. "You are so dead."

He barely made it out of the dining hall before he burst into laughter.

$\mathcal{I}$ watched Paton's every move carefully as he worked to light the fire in my bedchamber. I wanted to be able to do it myself if I ever needed to. He built the fire carefully, placing only two logs to burn so I'd have enough light and heat to get safely into bed, but not so much that it would keep burning well into the night.

"Thank you so much. I'm sure I could've managed it myself." It was a complete lie, but as this was surely a task anyone from this time could do in their sleep, I thought it best to pretend that I was equally as familiar with the process.

Righting himself as the flames grew, Paton turned to smile at me as he brushed away my thanks.

"No need, miss. Tonight 'twas my job. Tomorrow, Nicol will see the castle lit at night."

I smiled at his use of 'miss' when all of the other men would've said 'lass.' It confirmed what I already suspected. Paton was the baby of the group.

"Well, thank you all the same. Have a good night."

"Ye, as well. If ye need anything, I willna mind if ye wake me.

'Twould be better for ye to do that than go traipsing around the castle in the dark. There are far too many corridors for ye to get lost in unless ye are verra familiar with the castle. My room is at the bottom of the stairs, to the right."

As he closed the door behind him, I placed both hands on my hips and turned to look at the room and started to laugh. There was no way for me to brush my teeth or my hair—only a basin of cold water to splash over my face. While the thought of going to bed without brushing my teeth did ick me out a little, it was no bother to me that I would have to forgo my nightly ritual of proper skincare. A few days—or even weeks, for that matter—of a good water cleansing wouldn't kill me. What made me laugh was thinking of Marcus and the reaction I knew he must be having in his own room.

He was remarkably high-maintenance for someone with so little hair, and I knew having to pee in a small basin would horrify him.

Smiling to myself at the thought of Marcus stomping around his own room cursing everything and everyone in this castle, I washed my face as best I could, used the less-than-ideal facilities, and crawled into bed in my dress.

The bed was surprisingly soft and with the number of warm blankets spread on top, I found that while it was significantly lumpier than my modern memory foam bed, it wasn't uncomfortable in the least. What *was* uncomfortable was the binding of my dress. I knew I wouldn't be able to sleep with it on.

If every one of the men within the castle walls hadn't been perfectly respectable at dinner, I might have hesitated to strip down and sleep in the nude when there was no way to lock my door, but I knew Morna in a way that Marcus never would, thanks to the story she'd gifted me so many months ago, and I knew she wouldn't have placed me here if I was in any real danger.

Sighing with relief as I loosened the laces and allowed my

breasts to spring free, I shimmied out of the dress and crawled happily into bed.

I was lulled to sleep by the slowly dying fire.

---

*R*audrich could see nothing in the darkness of night. All he could make out was the faint glow of the moon. He couldn't see the road ahead or spot any branches that might be hanging down in his way on the forest path. He only knew they were drawing close from Pinkie's descriptions of what surrounded them.

Daylight was difficult enough, but once the sun went down, he caught glimpses of the fate he would face if the rest of The Eight were unable to heal him. The one hope he had was that his vision had not grown worse since leaving Allen territory, which meant that the progression of his blindness was indeed somehow connected to his time away from the castle and the fact that their spell of binding on the faerie buried below them was pulling more strength from him now that Timothy was gone.

Pinkie was a talented navigator, which more than made up for his bawdy language and incessant chattering. The man had as much stamina for riding as he did, which allowed them to ride more quickly and for longer stretches than he'd expected. He was worth more than the amount he'd paid him. The journey would've been entirely impossible without him.

"I believe we are here. I've never seen such gates in my life. Just who is it that ye are trying to keep out of here?"

Pulling his horse to a stop, Raudrich dismounted and, with his arms in front of him, carefully made his way over to the gate.

"These gates are not intended to keep others out. They are intended to keep a great evil in."

Pinkie laughed.

"Is it a three-eyed monster, then?"

Raudrich placed both palms on the gate as he felt around for the delicately hidden latch. "'Tis far worse. Surely, ye have heard the stories of this place?"

Pinkie's tone was surprised and more somber when he answered.

"Aye, o'course, but not many such stories are true."

Grasping the small lift that only The Eight knew was there, he felt the gate give way enough for him to push it open.

He was more certain of his steps on his way back to his horse. He knew the land around this castle like the back of his hand. He could make the remainder of the journey alone.

"Aye, well, the stories of this place are true."

Pinkie spoke quietly and Raudrich thought he detected fear in his tone.

"Ye are a druid, then? One of the mysterious Eight?"

Raudrich mounted his horse with ease.

"Aye, and here is where I must bid ye farewell. I've been away too long, and I doona know whether or not 'tis safe for ye beyond these gates." He reached for his bag of coins and tossed it toward Pinkie. "'Tis all that I owe ye, along with enough to see ye settled and fed in the village tonight."

Raudrich extended his hand and waited for Pinkie to shake his hand in farewell.

"Thank ye for this. It has been my pleasure to ride with ye these last days. If ye ever need my assistance again, ye know where to find me."

He waited until he could no longer hear the hooves of Pinkie's horse retreating back down the hill before pushing his way through the gate. After making sure it was securely closed behind him, Raudrich rode the rest of the way up to the castle.

The others wouldn't be expecting him for at least another three days, which was exactly as he preferred it. This way, he could slip quietly inside, retreat to his bedchamber, and get a thorough night's sleep before having to face the endless questions he knew they would all have for him.

Raudrich sighed as he dismounted once more and guided his horse into the stables. This was the only place in the world where he felt truly like himself. There were many troubles ahead of him, he knew. With Timothy gone, they all faced the arduous task of finding another druid worthy of replacing him, and he could already feel the power of the fae they kept locked away rising again. But all of that could be dealt with in a few day's time. For now, he had a long-awaited appointment with his sorely-missed bed.

He could feel the warmth of his blankets, could sense the sweet dreams he would have just thinking about it. He couldn't wait to crawl inside.

CHAPTER 13

*T*here was a residual feeling of warmth lingering in his bedchamber as he slipped inside and quietly closed the door—almost as if a fire had been lit inside not long ago.

Raudrich walked over to the fireplace and hovered his hands over the ashes. They were still warm.

Paton. It had to be Paton. He was the only one with reason to want to steal his bed. He couldn't even bring himself to blame him. The poor lad's own room was barely larger than a cupboard.

He held his breath and listened carefully. Within seconds, the soft rise and fall of someone breathing from under the covers reached his ears.

If he woke him, Paton would wake the rest of the men and the night of precious sleep he'd spent weeks longing for would be ruined. He'd be damned if he would be denied his own bed the first night after returning home in years.

Groaning, Raudrich walked over to the bed. Placing his hands on top of the blankets, he pushed the lad from the center of the bed over to one side so there would be room for him, as well.

The lad felt lighter than he expected. Perhaps, the pudgy

adolescent he'd known before he left had grown more slender in the past two years.

Paton let out a soft whimper as Raudrich moved him, and Raudrich couldn't suppress a laugh at the unusually high pitch of the sound.

Kicking off his shoes, Raudrich removed his riding shirt. With his riding breeches still on, he crawled inside and fell quickly to sleep.

I dreamt I was sleeping. The dream was spotty, and dark, and sexy as hell. I was in the arms of a man with my head snuggled against his broad, firm chest. He was warm and I was more comfortable in his hold than I could remember ever being in another's. I loved the way the stranger's hand—which came protectively around my back—cupped at my breast as we slept.

My head lifted and lowered with his chest as he breathed and his breath would lightly tickle my nose as he exhaled. Smiling, I slowly wound my right leg in between his broad thighs, pulling us even closer together.

My hand lay gently below his chest, and I allowed my thumb to swirl small circles on the tender side of his stomach.

His muscles tightened as he groaned.

It was a deep, sexy noise and my knee seemed to slide gently up and down the space between his legs on its own.

The slow rise and fall of his breath quickened as I felt him harden beneath the light touch of my knee.

My own breath came more quickly. As I breathed in, the smell of him—sweat and earth—reached my nostrils, and something at the edge of my mind began to tickle uncomfortably.

A thought was trying to break through, to break into my dream, but I fought against it. It was one of those dreams you never wanted to end, and as you feel morning coming, your conscious mind quietly urges your unconscious mind to just stay sleeping a little bit longer.

The man shifted beneath me, as his left hand came around and began to roam over my body. I moaned in response to his touch, and then the thought I'd been trying so desperately to ignore came soaring into my blissful dream.

This was *too* real—the warmth, the rise and fall of my head with his breath, the smell of him. It all slowly fell into place in my mind as I woke. I had no choice but to open my eyes.

It was still completely dark in the room and it took a long moment for me to wake enough for panic and terror to set in.

There was a man in my bed, and I was naked.

Shrieking, I raised and scooted to the edge of the bed, bringing my knees back until I kicked him in the side with so much force that he landed on the floor with a loud thud.

I continued to scream, then remembering that Marcus was only a room away, I began to call for him as I scuttled off the bed and pulled the mound of blankets onto the floor with me to cover myself.

The man I'd pushed to the floor began to scream, too. Not the same loud, panicked scream I was emitting, but a deep cry of pain and confusion.

The door to the bedchamber burst open. As I heard Marcus call out to me, I stopped screaming. If he was here, I was safe. I trusted Marcus with my life.

"Laurel! What's happening? Are you okay?"

Shaking, I stood and wrapped the blankets around me and held them tight with my arms.

"I woke to find one of them," I paused and pointed to the stranger who was now lifting himself off the floor, "in my bed."

In between groans, my assailant spoke.

"Paton, ye sound like a lassie. Why in God's name did ye kick me? Ye've broken at least one rib, I'm sure of it. And ye woke me from the bonniest dream."

Completely baffled, I walked around the edge of the bed to look down at him. His voice didn't match that of any of the men we'd met at dinner, and I couldn't deny that he sounded genuinely confused.

Just as he tried to stand, Marcus moved from the doorway and shoved him back to the ground.

"You stay right there, you son of a bitch, or I'll kill you."

I'd never heard Marcus so angry.

"Broken rib or not, I'd like to see ye try, lad." Pushing Marcus back with surprisingly little effort, the man did manage to stand. "Who the hell are ye, and what in the name of God is going on?"

Marcus held a lantern in his left hand and shoved it toward me just as he threw his right fist into the man's nose. The crack of it made my own nose hurt. There was no way it wasn't broken.

The impact sent the man tumbling backwards as the back of his head cracked against the stone wall a few feet behind him.

Just as the man crumpled to the ground, Harry, Ludo, and Quinn appeared in the doorway, each with a candle in hand.

Harry took one look at me and then at the man lying unconscious on the floor and quickly turned toward Marcus.

"Lad, I doona know what happened here, but I'm certain 'tis not how it appears. Take Laurel to yer room and tend to her. My men and I will tend to Raudrich, and I assure ye we will get to the truth of what happened here. If I am wrong about his character—if he did intend the lassie harm—ye can rest assured that we will see him duly punished for his crime."

Marcus was trembling with rage.

"Of course he meant her harm. He crawled into bed with her while she was sleeping. What else could he have meant?"

Harry's tone was sympathetic but he remained calm as he pointed to the unconscious man Quinn and Ludo were now lifting off the floor.

"He dinna know the two of ye were here, and 'tis his room that Laurel was sleeping in. Perhaps, he dinna know she was inside when he crawled in bed."

With the adrenaline slowing wearing off, I was able to think more clearly. I wasn't all that hard of a sleeper. If he'd tried to hurt me, I would've woken much sooner. And as loathe as I was to admit it, I could recall the beginning of my 'dream,' where I'd rolled toward him and slipped into the space between his arm and chest.

Gently, I stepped between Marcus and Harry and placed a light hand on Marcus' arm.

"I think he's right, Marcus. He didn't hurt me. It just scared me to death when I woke up and saw him. I thought…I thought I was dreaming. I truly do think this was just all a big mistake."

Marcus let out a breath that made me throw my arms around him in comfort. I knew what it felt like to be so worried for someone that when you learn they're okay, breath that you didn't even know you were holding comes out so quickly that it's hard to stay standing. It was the same way I'd felt when Mom had told me that Kate had woken from her coma.

His arms came around me quickly, holding the blankets up around me.

"Are you certain, Laurel? He didn't touch you? Didn't put his hands on you?"

There was no need for anyone else save me and this stranger to know the truth about just exactly how much touching had gone on.

"No. When I woke, I was on one side of the bed. He was on the other. It just scared me is all. I'm so sorry for causing this whole mess."

Harry placed a light hand on my back.

"This is my doing, lass. Calder was right when he said I shouldna have put ye in his room. I shall pay for it when Raudrich wakes. This is hardly the welcome he expected."

Marcus' voice was shaky but I knew he was satisfied that I was okay. He took one look at the blood pouring out of Raudrich's nose as Ludo and Quinn struggled to get him situated on the bed and winced.

"I'm sorry for hitting him."

Harry laughed and slowly ushered us out into the hallway.

"Doona be sorry, lad. Ye did what any good brother would do. Ye both need to rest after such a scare. We will see all of this settled come morning."

Marcus nodded and turned to lead me away.

We both knew we were done sleeping for the night.

CHAPTER 14

*R*audrich didn't know if he'd ever been in such pain before. There was no part of him that didn't ache dreadfully. He didn't care at all. He would gladly accept such pain forever for the blessing it had brought him.

He could see. Not as well as he once had, but so much better than the day before. The man to his left was more than a blurry blog. If he strained and looked past the swollen knob between his eyes, he could see that it was Maddock.

"What are ye smiling for? Ye really dinna need anything to make ye any uglier. Yer nose was large to begin with. It will be even larger when this heals."

Raudrich laughed but stopped abruptly at the sharp pain that shot through his side in response.

"I can see ye. Ye canna know how happy that makes me."

Maddock's brows pulled together in confusion and Raudrich delighted in the fact that he could see the gesture.

"What do ye mean? Marcus hit ye in the nose, he dinna poke yer eyes out."

"I'll tell ye all about it in a bit. First, I need one of ye to explain to me what happened last night. Who is the man that did this to me, and why did he wish to kill me?"

The entire night was a blur to him. It had been one of the happiest night's sleep of his life. He rarely dreamt of anything, but last night—on his first night home in far too long—he'd dreamt of a woman. Naked and pressed against him, he held her warm breast in his hand as her silky leg rubbed against his manhood, stirring him to arousal. It had all ended much too abruptly as Paton kicked him from the bed. The next thing he knew there was an angry voice in his ear and a fist flying toward his face. Then, everything went dark again.

Maddock shrugged.

"I doona have any idea. Harry willna tell me anything. I doona believe Nicol, Calder, or Paton even know ye are back yet. Harry woke me..."

Raudrich held his hand up to stop him.

"What do ye mean Paton doesna know I'm back yet? Was it not he that I found in my room last night?"

Maddock's eyes widened in understanding.

"Ach, no wonder he broke yer nose. Ye thought Paton was in yer bed?"

An uncomfortable sense of dread began to creep up his spine.

"Aye, 'tis what I said. 'Twas it not?"

Maddock started to grin.

"And ye crawled in bed with him?"

Raudrich nodded, his frustration growing.

"Aye. I was exhausted from the journey. I knew if I woke him, he'd wake the rest of ye and then I wouldna get to sleep until dawn."

Maddock shook his head and Raudrich could see he was suppressing laughter.

"Paton wasna in yer room last night."

"Then who the hell was?"

"Laurel."

Raudrich's body flooded with heat and horror. Was it possible that he'd not been dreaming? Had there truly been a lassie in his bed? Surely all that he'd felt—her skin, her breasts—it couldn't have been real? But if it was...had it been his doing or hers?

"Who is Laurel?"

"What do ye mean, who is Laurel? Ye've known her since ye were a child. She came all this way to see ye, though I doona believe she expected the greeting ye gave her."

He knew no one by the name of Laurel, but there were greater things on his mind.

"Is this Marcus her husband? Is that why he attacked me? He entered to find us asleep next to each other in the bed? I swear I thought 'twas Paton."

"Marcus is her brother, though not by blood."

The door to his room slowly creaked open as Harry stepped inside.

"Thank God, Harry. Ye were here last night, were ye not? Tell me what happened. Doona spare me anything."

Harry leaned over the bed and gave his leg a quick pat.

"Doona worry, Raudrich. All is well. The lass understands what happened and she isna angry with ye. She says that ye dinna touch her. She woke in the night to see ye lying on the other side of the bed and it gave her quite the fright. Ye can thank her for yer broken ribs. I just had Quinn ready a bath for her, but she'd like to speak to ye a bit later if ye doona mind. She's worried ye might be angry with her."

Angry with her? Her assumption made no sense to him. It was he who had crawled into bed with a naked woman and given her what must've been one of the greatest frights of her life. Accident or not, he owed the lass an apology.

"O'course I doona mind, but tell the lass I'm not angry with her. How could I be?"

Harry shrugged and turned to leave.

"I know. I told her that 'twas she who should be angry, but more than anything, I believe she is embarrassed."

"And she told ye that she knows me?"

Before answering him, Harry asked Maddock to bring him up some breakfast. The moment Maddock was gone, he leaned in close.

"Aye, though 'tis not true. Calder and I could tell straight away the moment we found her and Marcus out in our stables. She called ye the wrong name twice. She knows of ye, but I doona believe the two of ye have ever met. I thought it best to let the other men believe otherwise. Ye know most of them believe women to be a curse in this castle. If they thought her a stranger, they wouldna let her stay here. Because they believe she knows ye, they permitted it without question."

His curiosity for this woman grew with each new thing he learned about her.

"Ye found her in the stables? How did she get past the gate?"

"I doona know. It confounds me, though I doona believe she brings ill will. I quite like the lass, actually. Though, she has her secrets to be sure. I thought I would have time to try and learn them, but 'twas only yesterday morning that I found her."

"And what of Calder? He canna be pleased with this."

"He's not. But he willna say anything to the other men. He has his own secret that I keep for him."

Raudrich knew better than to ask.

"How bad does my face look, Harry?"

"I willna lie to ye. Ye look foul."

Harry turned to leave but called back to him as he left.

"I canna believe ye had a naked woman in yer bed and dinna know it. That must have been some journey. I doona believe I could ever be so tired."

CHAPTER 15

"*M*arcus…"

"Yes, Laurel?"

Marcus was sitting on the floor, his back against the side of the bed so that I was entirely shielded from his view as I bathed. He didn't want to be forced to answer questions about last night alone and I didn't want to be alone. I had to spill my secret shame to someone or I feared I would burst.

"I did a bad thing. A very bad thing."

"What could you have possibly done?"

He didn't sound like he believed me at all.

"You remember how I said that when I woke up, Raudrich and I were both on separate sides of the bed?"

"Yes. What about it?"

Thoroughly clean and freezing—the water had cooled quickly—I stepped out of the tub, dried myself off, and slipped back into my dress.

"Well, it wasn't exactly true."

"What?" Marcus flew off the floor and I had to run to block him from charging out the door.

"Hang on. Let me explain."

He was shaking again.

"What's there to explain? He either touched you or he didn't. Last night, you said he didn't. Now, you say he did. I'm back to wanting to kill him."

"Don't jump to a conclusion. There's a lot to explain, actually. You see," I couldn't even look at him while I said it. I stared down at my bare feet. "When I woke up, I was in his arms, my head on his chest, my legs intertwined with his. It was…intimate."

I glanced up at Marcus to gauge his reaction. He looked like he was about to blow a gasket. I held up a hand to stop him.

"Hang on. Let me finish. You see, I had a very interesting dream last night. At least, I thought it was a dream until I woke up in Raudrich's arms. Initially, I freaked out, which you already know. But what you don't know is that as I stood there watching you and Harry hash this out, I remembered something from the beginning of what I thought was a dream. Raudrich didn't initiate contact with me. I was the one who rolled over in the bed and snuggled into him. I touched him. He didn't touch me."

Marcus stepped back and moved to sit on the edge of the bed.

"Seriously?"

"Yes." I threw my hands up to cover my face. "I know I was sleeping, but still…I shamelessly felt him up. I even…" I hesitated and then lowered my voice as if I were worried the stone walls wouldn't keep my voice inside, "aroused him. Then I freaked out and broke his ribs."

A smile slowly spread across Marcus' face and as he silently crossed his arms and stared at me.

I dramatically slid down to the floor. "Why are you smiling?"

"You think this man will be angry about this?"

"Of course, he is."

Marcus shook his head.

"I'll admit that I'm sure he's not too pleased about the cracked ribs, but if you think he's upset you rubbed yourself against him, you know nothing about men. Besides, he was asleep until you kicked him off the bed. He may not even remember that you touched him."

That was true. Perhaps, I could get away with pretending nothing happened.

"You think?"

"Just go talk to him and say nothing to him about your sleep-induced fondling. Do you mean to apologize to him?"

An apology had never crossed my mind. I was embarrassed and felt guilty for what I'd done to him in my sleep, but I wasn't sorry. Accident or not, my reaction had been perfectly reasonable. What woman wouldn't have reacted in much the same way?

"No. I'm not going to apologize for kicking a man that crawled into bed with me while I was sleeping. I just need to talk to him. We both do, really, but I think it best if I visit with him alone first. I'm going to tell him what Morna told us to. And then we'll just," I shrugged, "see how he responds."

It was midday before the string of men stopped entering and exiting Raudrich's room on an endless rotation. Each of the men seemed anxious to visit with their friend who had been away for so long. I was also sure they all wanted to know exactly what happened last night. It was fine with me if they visited with him all day. I wasn't really looking forward to the awkward conversation.

After more than an hour of creepily hanging out in the hallway outside of his room, I finally worked up the nerve to knock. His response was immediate.

"Come in."

His voice sounded weary, and for a moment, I wondered if perhaps I should wait until another day to speak with him. He had to be exhausted, and there was no question that he was in pain.

Hesitantly, I stepped inside and said nothing for a few seconds as I looked him over. Even with his swollen nose and face, I could see that he was handsome. He sat propped up on the bed, with fabric wrapped tightly around his chest to help stabilize his ribs.

"Hi." I gave him a little wave, but stayed standing in the doorway. "I know you've had visitors all morning. I can come back later, or even tomorrow, if you'd rather."

He shook his head and waved me toward him.

"Nonsense, lass. I've been waiting for ye all morning. Do ye mind coming a little closer so I might tell ye how sorry I am, and so that I can properly see ye. Ye look like little more than a ghost from there."

I cocked my head to the side in confusion. The distance between us wasn't far at all. It couldn't be more than ten feet. Had Marcus truly hit him so hard, or was the man's vision naturally weak?

"Of course. It…it's not the injury that is making it difficult for you to see, is it?"

A chair sat right next to his bed, left there by the last man to visit with him. Following his gesture toward it, I took my seat next to him.

"No, though my nose is swollen enough that I do see more of it than anything else at the moment. I've been nearly blind for many weeks now. 'Tis healing though, now that I'm home."

That made absolutely no sense to me. I'd never heard of someone's vision improving based on location, but I said nothing of it. There were lots of things about the last few days that defied reasonable logic.

I decided it was best to start off with a proper introduction. I extended my hand.

"I'm Laurel."

He took it, and as he gripped my hand, I couldn't help but remember the way that same hand had felt cupped around my breast. My cheeks warmed at the thought, and I was certain my cheeks blushed. Thankfully, by the way he was squinting at me, I didn't think he could see it.

"I'm Raudrich." Releasing my hand, he began to apologize as I relaxed into the seat.

"Lass, I canna begin to tell ye how sorry I am for frightening ye last night. I promise ye, had I known that a lass was in my bed, I wouldna have entered it uninvited. As I told ye before, my vision is poor and at night, I canna see a thing. I did hear someone inside when I entered, but I truly thought it was Paton. I've been away from here for sometime. I thought perhaps he had decided to make himself at home in my chambers while I was away. If ye knew what his own room looks like, ye would understand why. In hindsight, I know that I should've awakened him to check, but we doona ever have lassies here. 'Tis a shock to me that Harry allowed ye entry. Ye must have charmed him more than ye know. I never dreamed that the person in my bed was someone I dinna know. I am sorry, lass."

His tone was remorseful, and I knew looking into his eyes that he meant every word. If I hadn't already been convinced of his innocence, his speech would've done the job.

"I know. There's no reason for you to be sorry."

He started to interrupt me, but as he leaned forward, the muscles across his chest tightened and he groaned at the sharp pain that ran through him. Taking in a pained breath, he leaned back into the pillows before speaking.

"There is much reason for me to be sorry. 'Tis bad enough that I entered the bed as ye slept. 'Tis another wrong entirely that I pulled ye against me. I swear to ye, I did so unconsciously in my sleep."

My breath caught uncomfortably. He did remember, then. Asleep or not, he was aware of the way we'd touched. In an uncomfortable panic, I set out to make him think otherwise.

"I don't know what you're talking about. You didn't pull me against you."

He smiled sympathetically.

"Lass, ye owe me nothing. Ye doona need to attempt to make me feel less guilty. I know I held ye in my arms."

"I'm not trying to make you feel anything. Our handshake was the first time we ever touched. When I woke up, I was on one side of the bed and you were on the other."

He didn't appear to believe me, but I could see by the way he started to speak but then bit his lower lip that he'd decided not to argue with me.

"If that is the way ye remember last night, I am glad of it, for I dinna care for the way I felt about myself this morning. The thought that I frightened ye or made ye feel unsafe wounded me greatly. I'm glad that we may put all that happened last night behind us."

I smiled and crossed my arms as I leaned back in the chair. With that discussion out of the way, I felt much more comfortable.

"Me, too."

He nodded in agreement and then took a deep breath before speaking once more. His tone this time was more direct, and far less friendly.

"Now, lass, forgive me for being so blunt, but why did ye lie to Harry? I doona know ye. I know with certainty I've never seen ye before in my life. So what are ye doing here, and how do ye know my real name?"

So much for being comfortable.

CHAPTER 16

*R*audrich watched Laurel closely as she shifted in the seat. She was beautiful. With blonde hair that fell just past her shoulders and thick, dark brows that framed icy blue eyes —even blurry—she was more attractive than he imagined she would be. It made his dream-like memories of the night before come to life in a way that made it impossible to deny what had happened.

He'd not been dreaming. When the lass had woken, she'd not been on the other side of the bed. Why then, did she wish to pretend that nothing had happened? He believed her when she said she wasn't trying to ease his guilt. What then wasn't she telling him?

There were so many things he wanted to ask her, but he thought it best to start with the most pertinent question. They all needed to know why she was here.

"Why…why am I here? Would you believe me if I told you that I'm not quite sure?"

He shifted and then cried out as the pain in his side ricocheted down his body. His damn ribs were going to be a problem. He didn't have time to lay in bed while they healed. He would have to call on the other men to use power they truly didn't have to spare to heal him. There was so much they all needed to do to protect their home and people now that Timothy was gone.

Before he knew it, Laurel's hands were on him. Gently she leaned toward him, placing her arms underneath his. Her movement was so intuitive, so natural, that he didn't question it as she spoke gently near his ear. The feel of her breath against his neck sent shivers down his spine.

"Here." she lifted him off the pillows, as she reached behind him to readjust him. "That doesn't look like the best position for those ribs." After a few moments of maneuvering, she released her grip and encouraged him to relax. "See if that is any better."

It was. He sighed as he relaxed into the greater support that was now built up behind his back.

"Aye, thank ye."

Smiling, she resumed her seat next to him.

"You're welcome. I'm sure you were about to tell me no—that you wouldn't believe me."

She was right. He didn't.

"Ye are not from this village. To come to our territory requires not only a long journey by horse, but also the short distance between this isle and the mainland by boat. Why would ye make such a journey if ye dinna know yer reason for doing so?"

Laurel sighed and leaned forward to rest her elbows on her knees as she spoke to him. It was a casual position and one he'd never seen a woman rest in. He found it rather endearing.

"You're going to think I'm crazy."

Laurel's accent was one he'd heard before. He sensed that if he could simply place it, so many answers about the strange woman would fall into place.

"Where are ye from, lass? Yer speech is uncommon, but I'm sure that I've heard it somewhere before."

Laurel's expression lifted, as if his acknowledgment gave her hope.

"Boston." She hesitated and then continued. "In…in the colonies."

"Ah."

It came to him in an instant. Sydney. Laurel's accent was much like Sydney's. In truth, she was like Sydney in many ways. They shared the same speech, the same casual mannerisms so different from most women he knew. He expected that if he was given a chance to know this woman more, he would find that she was as loose with her speech as Sydney was, as well.

Smiling, he thought of Harry's claim that they'd found her in the stables. The assumption that was forming in his mind truly was the only explanation.

"Are ye one of Morna's lassies?"

Laurel straightened and smiled as she pointed to him in her relief.

"Yes. Yes, Morna. That's what I was working up to, although I had no idea how you'd react. So you know her?"

Even before Sydney entered his life, he'd known of Morna. From the way his grandfather had always spoken of her, he wondered if perhaps he'd been in love with the witch. Though, for the sake of his grandmother, he'd never asked him outright.

"I've never met her, but she was a dear friend of my grandfather, and I know another lass she sent back."

Laurel looked immensely relieved.

"Oh, good. That must be why she left instructions to ask for you. So, you will believe me when I tell you that she sent Marcus and me two nights ago? We landed in your stables."

"Aye, lass, I believe ye." He chuckled as he thought of Sydney and all the other tales he'd heard of Morna's time-traveling lassies. "Are ye being truthful when ye tell me ye doona know why ye are here? I've only ever known of one reason for Morna to send lassies through time. She means to see ye matched with another."

He wondered if perhaps it might be him, and it shocked him to realize that the idea wasn't unappealing. God knew it had been too long since he'd taken a real fancy to any woman.

"Nope. That's not it this time."

He didn't quite care for the disappointment he felt at her quick dismissal.

"I know that's her usual thing, but she assured me that it wasn't this time. In all honesty, we didn't have time to get much explanation from her. She sort of sent us back against our will. She used some excuse that I might be able to get some ideas for my next book."

Curious, he interrupted her.

"Yer book, lass?"

Her cheeks blushed bright enough that he could see it through the fog of his vision.

"Yeah. I'm a writer. Or at least I used to be. It's been a while since I've been able to get myself to write anything."

He'd never known of a female to write before. Most didn't even know how to read. With so many opportunities for women in the time these lassies came from, he couldn't imagine how difficult it must be for each of them to wind up here.

"'Tis impressive, lass. What do ye write?"

She smiled and shook her head.

"It doesn't matter. In truth, I don't believe that's the real reason Morna sent us back here. I think it has something to do with my frie..." she hesitated and changed her wording. "With my brother, Marcus."

Raudrich had yet to meet this Marcus, though he already knew what the receiving end of his fist felt like, and he didn't wish to anger the man ever again.

"Why do ye say that?"

"Before I tell you, will you explain to me what the deal is with this place? I'd like to know how much of the legend is true."

He knew there were stories about him and the rest of The Eight throughout Scotland now, but it shocked him to hear that this woman—born centuries after all of them would be dead—knew anything about them at all.

"Do ye mean to say that in yer time—whenever that is—ye knew of us before ye came here?"

She nodded. "Yes. There are books written about you, even a documentary."

He had no idea what a documentary was.

"A documentary?"

"Nothing. I just want to know the real story, then I'll tell you my suspicions about Marcus."

It was such a long story—one that would take him far more energy to tell than he had now. And it would be easier to show her anyway. He needed sleep and to speak to all of the men alone. They'd yet to grieve Timothy together, and they needed to form a plan on how they would begin the search for the next druid.

"I'll happily tell ye, lass, but not just now. Might I find ye later? I promise ye I'll tell ye all of it then."

She stood and smiled. She had the prettiest smile—warm and friendly—and it had a slightly mischievous look to it that made her even more alluring.

"Okay. I'll hold you to that. You need to rest anyway. It was lovely to meet you, Raudrich."

As she left him, he couldn't help but think about how unexpectedly lovely it was to meet her, as well.

His life suddenly felt very different, like with one simple introduction, things would never be the same.

Good or bad, he didn't yet know.

CHAPTER 17

I'd wanted to speak to Raudrich alone in the hopes of getting the real story about this castle and the interesting men within it without Marcus being present. If even part of the story I'd watched with Kate was true, if the book was to be believed, Marcus' reason for being here would have a lasting impact on the history of this castle and territory. I knew Marcus well enough to know that he wouldn't be receptive to such news.

He loved his life back in Boston—even with the recent downturn in his freelance photography business. While I was his best friend, he had many others, as well. And he was even closer to his family than I was to Kate. He was a modern man. He didn't share my same passion for all things old. Scotland didn't seem to call to his soul like it did mine.

Was it possible that Marcus was indeed a druid? Did he have powers just waiting to be brought to life inside of him? If so, I knew he was entirely unaware of it.

I found myself wishing that I'd taken the time to actually read the book that had fallen from my shelf. In the surprising turn of events that occurred that night, I'd not thought much of the book as we packed to leave. I regretted being so thoughtless now.

At some point in history, the supposed curse on this land must have been broken. For if not, I imagined the Eight Lairds would still split the land equally in my own time. From what I'd read online about visiting the castle in modern times, this wasn't the case. What I didn't know was at what point in history the curse was broken. Was it soon—as in the following weeks while Marcus and I would be here? If so, perhaps it was possible that Marcus could become one of The Eight, help to break the curse, and then return home. But, what if the curse was to live on in this land for another generation or two? If that was the case, and Marcus was destined to be one of The Eight, did that mean he would have to stay here forever?

I'd said nothing to Marcus about any of it, and I had no plans to until I had more information at my disposal. To do so would only make him more eager to find a way to return home. Something I seriously doubted would be possible until we'd fulfilled whatever Morna believed we were meant to.

Besides, so far I'd seen no indication that any of The Eight were capable of magic. I knew it was very likely that once Raudrich was rested enough to tell me the truth, I would learn that much of what had become legend in my own time would be untrue.

Since I knew I would be waiting around impatiently for Raudrich unless I found something to occupy my mind and time, I decided to go in search of some writing materials. While no clear story was yet in mind, I could at least start taking some notes and see where my brainstorming might lead.

Most of the castle corridors were quiet, much like the day before. The men of this castle worked hard, and it didn't surprise me that I had difficulty finding one of them about.

After searching most of the second floor, I made my way

downstairs where I could hear the faint sound of voices from a dark corridor I'd yet to explore.

Remembering Harry's directive that we were free to roam as we pleased, I followed the noise to the top of another stairwell. Two voices—one I recognized as Calder's—were speaking down below.

Not wishing to eavesdrop, I called out to them right away.

"Hello? Is it all right if I come down?"

The voice that wasn't Calder's answered back. "Aye, o'course. Calder and I were just trying to find the source of the foul smell down here. Mayhap ye could help us?"

I could smell nothing from where I stood, but as I made my way down into the dank storage room, the scent of rot reached me. I pinched my nostrils closed to block it.

"Wow. That is rather bad, isn't it?"

Maddock stood at the entryway to the small storage room and held up the lantern so I would have some light as I descended the last few steps.

"Aye, lass. I keep telling Calder 'tis likely that moisture got into one of our barrels and ruined food, but his imagination has run away from him. He believes something more nefarious is at work."

I looked over at Calder to see him staring at Maddock with annoyance before turning angry eyes toward me.

"This is yer fault, lass. Ye have no business here. 'Twas clear enough from the moment I met ye that ye were a liar. Now ye have placed us all in danger. Ye and yer brother—if he truly is that—need to leave. Now."

Stunned, I stepped back against the cold wall behind me. I knew Calder was weary of our presence here, but until now, he'd at least been cordial. Something in his eyes was different now, and I didn't like his gaze at all.

Before I could say a word, Maddock stepped between me and Calder.

"Shut yer mouth, ye rude bastard. We doona even know what the source of the smell down here is. 'Tis a natural occurrence, I'm certain. Doona place this on her. Time away from polite society has ruined yer manners."

Calder stepped very close to Maddock, and his tone was filled with venom as he spoke. "Look around, Maddock. Open every storage barrel. Ye will find the same as I did. I spent all morning searching. Nothing is rotting. 'Tis Machara's anger rising from her tomb. Ye know as well as I that it willna be long before she begins to act out. Timothy's death was enough to strengthen her. A lassie's presence will give her even more power. I doona care if the rest of ye are so lust-crazed that ye are willing to damn us all just so ye can stare at a woman for a few days. She's not worth it, Maddock. I might understand if she were pretty, but ye all know she is not. She's got more padding on her than half our pigs. Ye are all ignorant fools, and I willna placate a one of ye."

If he'd said such insulting words directly to me it would've been bad enough, but the fact that he was saying it about me—right in front of me—somehow made it worse.

I'd never been small or particularly slender. I was tall for a woman, and my stature would never be described as delicate. I was undoubtedly thicker—curvier—than what modern-day media would have people believe was "beautiful," but in truth, I was no larger than the average woman. For much of my life, it had been my greatest source of insecurity, especially since Kate's perfect figure had been the envy of every girl we knew growing up.

For me, those thirty extra pounds were something that ate at my confidence and led me to believe that I deserved less of everything than I did. Less money, fewer friends, less love, fewer experiences. It took me most of my twenties to get to a place where I could see that every self-depreciating belief I held about myself was a lie.

Perhaps, someday I would lose the weight. Perhaps not. Either way, my size fourteen jeans were still the least interesting thing about me.

At least, I thought I'd evolved enough for such words not to hurt me. Calder's words made me think differently. With his few thoughtless sentences, it felt like high school all over again—like standing in the locker room hearing the jeers and whispers of anorexic-looking brats. I had half a mind to tap him on the shoulder and then shove his balls halfway up his ass with my knee for being such an asshole, but while I was still reeling from his words, Maddock grabbed Calder by the throat and threw him up against the wall with so much force that I wouldn't have been surprised if his head was now cracked and bleeding in the back.

Unfortunately, it wasn't.

"I doona know what has gotten into ye, but fear has made ye someone I'm ashamed to know. Get out of my face before I break yer neck. If I see ye anywhere near Laurel or Marcus for the rest of the time they are here with us, I shall see ye sent away from this castle for good."

I could see by the look in Calder's eyes as Maddock stepped away that he knew his threat wasn't an empty one. Leaving Calder trembling against the wall, Maddock took my hand and quickly ushered me back upstairs.

The moment we were in the light-filled grand corridor of the castle, Maddock looked at me. Whether it was intuition or my quickly-reddening face, he knew I was about to cry.

"Come here, lass."

Even once we're grown, we all carry wounds that when poked cause us pain.

In a few hours, I would be fine, but for now, I couldn't deny how hurt I felt.

I allowed Maddock to pull me into his arms as I wept.

CHAPTER 18

"What do ye mean Calder is gone? Do ye mean to the village? When will he be back? He knows 'twill require all of ye to heal me."

Maddock's jaw was clenched, his eyes narrow. Raudrich was half-surprised that steam wasn't coming out of his ears. Maddock was one of the most calm and centered men among them. Raudrich had never seen him so angry.

"No, I doona mean to the village. His horse and satchel and every personal item he had are no longer in the castle. I followed him to see if he would truly go through with it, and he has. He loaded himself and his horse on a boat and left the isle completely. He has abandoned his post here and us along with it."

Raudrich couldn't believe what he was hearing. They couldn't afford to lose another man.

"And why dinna ye stop him?"

Maddock's tone was entirely without remorse, "If that arse of a man wants to leave us, then good riddance to him. I thought I knew him. 'Twas clear to me earlier today that I dinna know him at all. He is not the sort of man we need here with us. If ye'd heard what I heard, ye would've not only let him leave, ye would've taken him down to the shore and thrown him in a boat yerself."

"What did ye hear?"

Just as Maddock opened his mouth to answer him, Harry, Ludo, Quinn, and Paton entered his bedchamber. Nicol was still sleeping, as he did every day until dinner.

"Maddock, we hoped ye were already in here. Where is Calder? We've much to discuss while Quinn's stew cooks away in the kitchen."

Raudrich barely listened as Maddock told the rest of them what he'd just told him. His mind was now too busy wondering what this would mean. Was it even possible for one of The Eight to leave, to break their bond of their own accord? It had never been something they'd had to worry about before now. If there was a way for Calder to remove his magic from its bind to the isle, what would happen when The Eight became Six?

He was deep in thought when Quinn reached out and grabbed his arm.

"Are ye here, Raudrich? Did ye hear a word we said?"

"No." He shook his head as he shifted in his bed. It was impossible to get comfortable with the ache in his ribs. "I dinna. I'm sorry. Calder's departure means bad things for all of us."

Quinn nodded as they all gathered around his bed.

"Aye, there is no question about that, but we doona have the luxury of dwelling on it. Nor, do we have the time to mourn Timothy's death with ye as we wished to. As ye know, we saw him buried shortly after his death. Ye must say goodbye to him on yer own time now."

He'd hoped they would all have a chance to reminisce about their old friend, to bid him farewell properly, but Raudrich understood Quinn's urgency. With each new event at the castle, their time became all the more precious.

"Aye, I shall visit his grave as soon as I can walk without crying out in pain, which I'm afraid may be weeks now that Calder is gone."

"No."

Harry's sure voice surprised him. Healing magic was exhausting. With his magic too weakened by the frail state of his body, they couldn't risk the strain that such an act would place on the remaining five.

"What do ye mean, no? I'll heal as quickly as I can, but I doona know how I can rush it."

Harry sat down on the edge of the bed. Raudrich could see by the stern gaze in his eyes that his mind was already made up.

"We canna wait weeks for ye to heal. If Calder truly means to leave, he will begin to look for a way to break his bind with us. Should he succeed before ye are healed, none of us can know the strength it would give Machara. 'Tis better for us to all let our magic be weakened for a day or two now than for us to be without the magic of three of the eight in a few weeks time. Ye willna be able to wield all of yer own power until yer body is healed. We shall pool our energy now and make tomorrow a day of rest for all of us so we might regain our strength before we determine what must be done next."

Raudrich couldn't deny that such a plan appealed to him. He wanted his body back, and if they could, his sight, as well.

"If ye all wish to do this, I willna fight ye on it. With my eyes, and now this, I havena felt like myself for far too long. Timothy's death has placed a strain on all our magic. It willna take long for Calder to begin to feel the ill-effects of being away from the castle."

Maddock's angry voice spoke beside him.

"Then may he lose his sight completely and much more quickly than ye lost yers."

All of the men looked at Maddock in question, but before he could say more, Harry stood.

"Then, let us begin, lads. Should this work, Raudrich, ye may have to be the one to finish dinner for I doona know if the rest of us will be able to stay standing afterwards."

Raudrich laughed as the men formed the necessary circle around him.

"If ye succeed at healing my ribs, my nose, and my sight, I shall wait on ye all hand and foot for a fortnight, at least."

Ludo laughed and Raudrich shifted so he could lie down completely on the bed. The healing was bound to be unpleasant, and he needed to prepare himself for the pain.

"Doona make promises ye have no intention of keeping. We all know that by this time tomorrow, ye will be ordering us about. Ye will have no sympathy for our exhaustion."

Ludo was probably right about that. Serving as laird for the past two years in Allen territory had made him bossy. It would take time for him to grow used to an equal partnership with the other men again.

Energy built in the room as they started to chant. It didn't take long for the pain to begin to sear through his body. Try as he might to swallow his screams, they wouldn't stay inside him.

It was horrific. No matter how much he screamed at them to stop, they continued their chant.

He wished he would pass out, but as the pain raged on, he remained awake, feeling the shift of every bone and every pull of his skin.

Only as his vision cleared and he was able to make out the beams across the ceiling was he able to relax into the pain.

As soon as they were finished, it would all be worth it.

CHAPTER 19

True to his word, Raudrich worked in the kitchen finishing their meal while the rest of the men rested. He had more energy than he'd had in months.

His ribs were still sore—a garish bruise spread all the way down his left side—but blessedly, they were no longer broken. His nose was as straight as it ever had been, and his vision was completely healed.

The only thing putting a damper on his mood was the anticipation of the hard time the men would give him over the quality of their meal. He'd not had cooking duty in over two years, and it showed.

The bread was edible, but chewy. The stew was too salty and the meat within it too tough. His hope was that they would all be too tired to care about what a poor job he'd done finishing Quinn's stew.

"I willna be surprised if Harry sleeps through dinner. I could hear his snores from the other side of the castle."

Raudrich looked up to see Maddock enter the kitchen. The man looked dead on his feet, wobbly and unsteady as he walked toward him.

"Take a seat, man. Ye should be in bed yerself. I told ye all I would come to fetch ye when 'twas ready."

"Ach." Maddock waved a dismissive hand but took a seat on the wooden stool that sat beside the large wooden preparation table. "I'm still too angry to sleep."

So relieved at his recovery, Raudrich had been able to put thoughts of Calder aside for a short while. Maddock's words immediately brought the questions he'd had before the healing session back to him.

"Ye never did tell me. What did he do? What did ye hear him say?"

Maddock leaned into the table for support as he spoke.

"I'll not tell the other men. 'Twould embarrass Laurel if she heard of it, and I doona wish to betray her trust. But seeing as ye've known her so long, I thought it best ye hear what was done to her."

Raudrich didn't bother correcting Maddock. It was fine with him if all save Harry believed he and Laurel had a history. It would allow him to spend more time with her without questions arising from the other men. He barely knew the lass, none of them did, but he very much wanted to know more about her.

Whatever he'd expected, it had never crossed his mind that what had happened with Calder had anything to do with Laurel. The sense of protectiveness he felt come over him at knowing Calder had wronged her, surprised him immensely.

"Laurel? What does she have to do with this?"

"It has everything to do with Laurel. He all but attacked her, and when I stepped in to chide him for it, he said things about her that I wouldna say to a dog. I wanted to kill him. Truly, I did."

"What did he say?"

Maddock shook his head and exhaled sadly.

"Ach, Raudrich, ye should've seen her face. She looked like a child her expression was so wounded. I doona think I shall ever be able to forget it. Not that I blame her for being hurt. His tone was so cruel and his words unjust in every way."

Raudrich quickly grew impatient.

"For the love o'God, man, what did he say to her?"

"He dinna say it to her, which, if ye ask me, made it even more unkind. He spoke to me, though he knew good and well she could hear every word. She was standing right next to us."

Raudrich dropped the knife in his hand dramatically and crossed his arms as he stared at Maddock, silently urging him to continue.

"He said that 'twas bad luck that she was here, that only bad things would come from it, and that the only reason we permitted her being here was because we were filled with lust and enjoyed having a lassie about. Then he said she was too full-figured to be pretty and that we were damned fools. He said that half our pigs were less pudgy. 'Twas unnecessary and cruel. Most men would've simply decked him, but ye know as well as I how such words would wound a woman. She did nothing to deserve his cruelty."

Raudrich knew he should've felt angry, but confusion was pushing any other emotion away.

"What the hell is he talking about? I doona believe I've ever seen a woman whose appearance I fancied more than Laurel's."

The confession slipped out of him, and he immediately regretted his honesty as he saw Maddock smile.

"Well, I'm certain she will be glad to hear it. Her brother claims she's in love with ye. But I..."

Stunned, he interrupted Maddock.

"In love with me?"

Maddock, wide-eyed and smiling, nodded.

"Aye. She hasna yet told ye, then? Well, pretend ye are surprised when she does. I wouldna want her thinking I spoiled her admission."

Maddock was clearly under a false assumption, but he could see no reason to correct him.

"I dinna mean to interrupt ye, ye just surprised me, is all. What were ye about to say?"

He sat quietly for a moment as if he were trying to remember. Then he shook his head as it came back to him.

"Oh, I was just going to agree with ye. While I suppose such a scrawny, unfortunate looking bastard like Calder would prefer a lass small enough to make him feel like more of a man, I doona mind a lassie with more meat on her bones. I find Laurel verra bonny, as well. I believe ye would be hard pressed to find a man who shares Calder's opinion of her."

Even Maddock's suggestion surprised him. While he knew his vision had still been impaired when he visited with Laurel, her size had never crossed his mind. More than that, he could still remember what it felt like to hold her in his arms. He'd never found the feel of someone against him more pleasing.

"Calder is an imbecile and I am glad we are rid of him." Raudrich paused and brushed his hands on his pants. "Now, let us put all of this nastiness behind us, for I doona like such talk of Laurel even between us. She deserves more respect than to be whispered about amongst men."

Maddock stood and nodded in agreement.

"Aye, 'tis precisely why I will say nothing of this to the other men. 'Tis only that I willna be surprised if she still seems rattled by the whole ordeal over dinner. I dinna want ye asking her what was wrong in front of everyone else, so I thought I should tell ye."

If Laurel's belief in her own beauty was in any way damaged by Calder's idiocy, he would make certain that her confidence was restored.

"I'm glad ye did. Do ye have the strength to go and gather the others for dinner, or should I?"

Maddock sank bank down onto the stool.

"If I walk back up those stairs again, I willna have the strength to come back down them for dinner. Best ye go."

Raudrich smiled. He expected his friend was milking the situation just a little.

"Aye, fine. Go and rest yerself at the table. I'll gather everyone now."

CHAPTER 20

"*I* can wait if you want, Laurel. It's really not a big deal."

Marcus was eyeing me skeptically. He could see that something was wrong. While he knew better than to ask, I could see that it annoyed him that I'd yet to tell him what was up with me.

I didn't want to talk about it. Not with Marcus. Not with anyone.

It had taken an hour-long walk, three failed attempts at meditation, and some serious positive self-talk to gain my composure. I'd actually been thankful for the screaming—terrifying as the sound was with the way it echoed down every hallway in the castle—when it began. It helped me block out my own self-pity-filled thoughts. By the time the mysterious screaming finished, I was in a much better mood.

"No, it's okay. Go ahead and go down. I'm just going to finish braiding my hair. I'll be down in just a minute."

I wanted a few minutes to myself before dinner. I needed to take a few deep breaths and figure out how I was going to manage to sit across from Calder without lunging across the table at him or collapsing into tears again.

Maddock had been nothing but the perfect gentlemen—understanding and tender as he'd held me and allowed me to cry. He'd also hit on me in the absolute kindest way I'd ever been hit on in my life, but I'd not read into that overmuch. It was a pity come-on, but I still appreciated it, all the same.

Marcus hesitated as he reached the doorway.

"Do you think it's safe? What do you think that screaming was?"

While part of me hoped the screaming was a result of Maddock hooking Calder up to some horrifying torture device, I knew his rude words weren't enough to deserve such pain.

"I'm not sure, but I suspect maybe they came from Raudrich. I don't know how medical stuff works around here, but if they were trying to set his ribs or his nose or something, that must have hurt like a son of a bitch."

Marcus bared his teeth sympathetically.

"Ouch. I really do need to apologize to the guy. Can't say I'm looking forward to that interaction."

If Raudrich's interaction with me was any indicator of his true character—which I had a feeling it was—he would be perfectly receptive to Marcus' apology.

"Maybe after dinner you can go and see him. He'll be kind to you, I'm sure. You'll feel better once you get it out of the way."

He nodded and opened the door to leave me.

"You're right. Don't take too long. I don't want to field dinner-time questions from everyone without you."

Once the door closed behind him, I quickly finished the loose braid at the nape of my neck and allowed it to drape over my left shoulder.

I never braided my hair back home, but something about it felt century-appropriate regardless whether or not that was actually true.

Taking a glimpse of myself in the mirror, I felt a little bit better than I had all day. Calder was entitled to his opinion. It didn't make it true. My breasts looked awesome in this dress, and my extra 'padding' as Calder had said, gave me a comely shape that I quite liked. I had a pretty face and smile, and as far as I was concerned, Calder had the face of a constipated pug. I was certain I had far less time picking up men than he did women.

"Screw him."

I whispered the words under my breath just as someone began to knock on the door to the bedchamber. Dread filled me. If it was Calder, I didn't want to answer. I didn't need his apology. I didn't need to ever speak to him again. Smoothing my dress and straightening my shoulders, I cautiously walked over to the door.

"Who is it?"

"'Tis Raudrich, lass. I came to fetch ye for dinner."

"Raudrich?"

I was so surprised to hear his voice on the other side of the door that I flung the door open so quickly, it nearly hit me in the head. As I looked back at him, I reeled back in shock.

"Wha…Wha…How? You look great."

It was nearly as baffling to me as the time travel. Raudrich had looked absolutely awful only a few hours earlier, now he looked unnervingly hot.

His bloodied and swollen nose was healed, and from the way he stood, I didn't believe his ribs were hurting him any longer.

He also was no longer squinting, almost as if he could see perfectly well.

He smiled at what I knew had to be my bug-eyed expression.

"Ye do know that we are druids, lass? Dinna ye hear me screaming? They healed me."

So that part of the legend was true. I could mark one question off of my very long list.

"Um, yes, yes I definitely did hear you screaming, but I never imagined that they were doing all of that." I motioned up and down his body with my hand, and he laughed.

"Ye approve then? I look fair better than I did before, aye?"

"You still looked pretty good before, too, but now you look...wow."

The moment I heard the words leave my mouth, I nearly fell back in shock. What the freaking hell had gotten into me? I could feel the blood rush to my face as I warmed into a horrifyingly embarrassing blush.

Thankfully, he said nothing to embarrass me further and gracefully moved on to another topic of conversation.

"I hope ye are not overly hungry. The lads are all rather tired after the spell they did for me so I was forced to finish the meal. It has been some time since I cooked. 'Tis rubbish."

I was famished, but I wouldn't tell him that.

"I'm sure it will be fine. Is everyone else already down there? I'm sorry if you all were waiting on me. You really should have just gone on ahead."

"All save Calder are on their way downstairs now."

At the mention of Calder's name, my smile fell. I hoped that Raudrich didn't know about what happened. I tried to keep my tone as congenial as possible as I asked about him.

"Why isn't Calder going to dinner?"

"He's gone, lass."

"Gone?"

I couldn't tell from his expression whether he knew about what had happened or not. He was totally unreadable.

"Aye. We doona expect that he will return."

"Oh." It felt as if a weight had lifted from my chest. I was beyond glad that I wouldn't have to see him again.

He offered me his arm and I took it as we made our way downstairs.

"Do ye still wish to know the truth of this place?"

I nodded as I looked up into his dark brown eyes.

"Of course, I do."

"After dinner, come and wait for me on the stairs. I must make certain that Nicol is out of the castle before I show ye. Once he is gone, I'll come to get ye."

I couldn't wait for dinner to be over.

CHAPTER 21

*S*eeing her now, laughing at one of Ludo's very un-funny jokes, her blue eyes twinkling in the candlelight, he knew one thing with certainty: he wasn't the one with unwell eyes, Calder was as blind as a bat.

Raudrich already knew he thought her beautiful, but with his sight fully restored, Laurel truly did take his breath away.

She seemed to be having a similar effect on Maddock, and Raudrich didn't care for it at all. The man stared at her with doe-like eyes as he laughed and smiled right along with her. For a group of men who were supposedly so weak from using their magic on him, not a one of them was having a problem conversing with her.

He and Marcus seemed to be the only one's not enjoying dinner with the same joyous abandon as the rest of them. They sat awkwardly next to one another, neither of them saying a word until Marcus finally leaned over to speak halfway through dinner.

"Uh...I suppose it's time that I introduce myself to you. I'm Marcus."

Raudrich gladly took the man's hand. He needed a distraction from watching the other men fawn all over Laurel.

"Raudrich. I am sorry I was not here to greet the two of ye when ye arrived."

Marcus snorted and withdrew his hand.

"I'm sorry you weren't here, too. If you had been, I wouldn't have had reason to punch you in the nose. By the way, I really am sorry about that. I mean, if it had been how it appeared, I wouldn't be sorry at all, but seeing that it wasn't, I do regret breaking your nose."

Raudrich pointed to his nose and smiled. "No worries, lad. As ye can see, 'tis fixed well enough now."

Marcus nodded. "Good. I'm glad there are no hard feelings."

"None at all. Ye were right to defend Laurel in such a way." He looked across the table and glared as Maddock reached out to touch Laurel's hand as he spoke to her. "I can assure ye, I would do the same if I saw anyone place an unwanted hand on her."

He was tempted to smash Maddock's nose in right this second.

Marcus followed his gaze and laughed.

"She's oblivious to it, you know. She knows so much about love in her writing and so little about it in real life. I've watched grown men trip over themselves trying to get her attention, and she doesn't notice."

Marcus' insight into Laurel was enough to pull his attention away from the soon-to-be-sorry Maddock.

"Love in her writing? Does she write poetry?"

"No. She writes romance novels."

He'd never heard of such a thing.

"Romance novels?"

Understanding moved across Marcus' face as he lowered his voice.

"Did Laurel tell you...do you know where or more precisely, when we are from?"

Raudrich responded in kind by leaning closer to Marcus. None of the other men knew.

"Aye, lad, I know all about Morna and her penchant for sending lassies through time."

"Good. Anyway, I'm pretty certain romance novels don't exist in this time. It will take quite a long time before women start really owning their sexuality."

Raudrich liked the sound of that very much. He thought perhaps he would like the future.

When he said nothing, Marcus continued.

"She writes love stories. You know, stories about men and women falling in love."

"But ye say that she knows little of this herself?"

The man snorted again. He wondered if perhaps it was a nervous habit, although nothing about the way the man held himself indicated that he was intimidated, and he'd certainly not behaved that way last night

"Laurel? God, no. She dates because her sister forces her to, but I've never known Laurel to be with a man for more than a few months. She's very distrusting of men, and she's a bit of a heartbreaker, but like I said, she doesn't see it. I'd say nearly all of the men she's ever dated have fallen for her by date three. But as soon as she sees them start to invest, she flees. I know her better than anyone, and I've never been able to determine exactly why."

Each new thing he learned about her made him even more curious to get to know her. It was time for their dinner to come to an end.

Standing, he pushed back from the table and addressed the group.

"It has been a long day for us all. If everyone is finished, I believe it best we all find our way to bed."

Even as riveted as the men seemed to be in their conversation, all of them agreed that they were indeed tired. As the men stood, he winked at Laurel to acknowledge their upcoming meeting.

Turning, he left to head for the castle's highest tower where he could watch for Nicol's nightly exit.

---

*T*ry as I might to convince Maddock that it really would be fine for me to bunk with Marcus, my new friend wouldn't hear of it. So, rather than wait on the stairs like I promised Raudrich I would do, I was forced to follow Maddock up to his bedchamber, while he chatted away about why this was the best solution for everyone.

"I promise ye, lass, 'tis no trouble at all. I willna place ye in Calder's room on the off chance that he might return, but I've no problem confronting him if he does, so I will stay in there. Even more, my bedchamber is one of only two that has a lock that ye may bolt from the inside. I've been known to walk about in my sleep, ye see. So I lock it before bed to keep myself inside. Doona want to go tumbling down the stairs in the night, aye?"

While I appreciated his kindness, it was ridiculous for so many people to be unsettled due to our invasive arrival into their lives. Marcus and I had shared rooms on countless trips and sleepovers.

"Maddock, I truly do appreciate your thoughtfulness, but I wouldn't be able to live with myself if I woke to hear that you'd walked out of Calder's room in the middle of the night and broken your leg by doing what you just told me you feared."

Just as we turned the corner down the long corridor leading to Maddock's bedchamber, Raudrich appeared from a set of stairs to my right. He stopped short when he saw us and slowly glanced back and forth between us.

"What are ye doing, Maddock?"

I couldn't understand the frustrated glint in Raudrich's eyes.

"I'm seeing Laurel to my bedchamber."

Frustration turned to anger in a flash, and before I knew it, Raudrich had stepped between us as he shoved Maddock with one hand and grabbed my arm with another.

"Like hell ye are, Maddock."

Raudrich turned his angry eyes on me, and I pulled out of his grasp as he spoke.

"Lass, I know Maddock can be verra convincing with his words, but ye doona want to do this. Ye barely know him. He is not the man for ye."

Maddock burst into laughter.

"Careful, Raudrich, yer envy is showing. I wasna leading her to my bedchamber to bed her, ye daft fool. I thought mayhap since my room has a lock, she could stay there while I move to Calder's. Laurel and I shall be bonny friends, I'm sure of it, but I doona think we shall ever be more. Right, lass?"

A blush blossomed underneath Raudrich's rather tan and weathered skin, and I couldn't help but grin at how boyish he looked when embarrassed. It made me feel better about the idiotic compliment I'd given him earlier.

I nodded emphatically. I liked Maddock immensely, but I wasn't interested in him in the least.

"Right. All the same though, as I was saying to you before, I don't need to stay in your room. I'll stay with Marcus."

"No." Raudrich recovered quickly from his embarrassment and turned to look me straight on.

"Ye willna stay with Marcus, nor will ye stay in Maddock's room, for Maddock will kill himself traipsing around in the night if he isna locked up inside. Ye will stay in my room for 'tis the nicest and is precisely where a lady like ye should be. I'll put a bolt on it before bed. I shall move to Calder's room."

I had rather liked Raudrich's room a lot.

"Okay, great. Thanks anyway, Maddock. Now, let me go and tell Marcus where I'll be staying. I'll meet up with you in a bit."

I turned and left both men to finish their arguing alone.

CHAPTER 22

$\mathcal{R}$audrich was waiting for me on the stairs by the time I finished explaining to Marcus what I was doing and where I would be staying tonight. He wanted to come with me, but I talked him out of it by claiming that I thought I would be more likely to get more information out of him alone. It wasn't true. I had no doubt that Raudrich would be just as willing to tell Marcus everything as he was me, but I wanted the opportunity to learn the truth on my own, so I could know just what it meant for my very best friend and the rest of his life.

"I'm sorry for earlier, lass. 'Tis not my place to tell ye who ye should spend yer time with. 'Tis only that it was a shock for me to see ye heading to Maddock's room with him. He's not good enough for ye."

I smiled and accepted his apology with a wave of my hand.

"It's fine. Although, I have to disagree with you on behalf of Maddock. I'm a hard sell when it comes to most men. Maddock is one of the good ones."

Raudrich raised his brows but nodded in agreement.

"Mayhap so, lass. It doesna mean ye should be with him."

I'd blown off Maddock's mocking of Raudrich earlier, but just now I couldn't deny that his tone did sound slightly jealous. Of what exactly, I couldn't imagine. He didn't know me well enough to be jealous of anything.

"You're right. Now, enough talk about me. I've had questions stirring inside me all day. Where does Nicol go at night, and why did we have to wait until he was gone to discuss this?"

Raudrich bent so that his face was right next to mine. Quietly, he whispered in my ear, and I had to reach for the handrail to stay steady. His breath against my neck brought up memories of the night before.

"Do ye trust me, lass? It will be easier for me to show ye than tell ye, but to do so requires that we travel somewhere ye willna like at all."

It surprised me to realize that I did trust him. While I had no real reason, I just intuitively felt that I would be safe with him.

"I think so. Show me and we'll find out."

He extended his hand. The moment I latched on, he turned and walked back up the stairs. I had to move quickly to keep up with him.

"I doona wish ye to think that I am doing anything Nicol would disapprove of. He wouldna mind me showing ye. 'Tis only that I prefer to do so without his knowledge for I know how much it pains him to speak of it."

With the castle already down for the night, no flames were lit along the hallways. I didn't realize until we turned down a dark corridor around the corner from Raudrich's bedroom that neither of us had any lighting. The hallway was lined with windows, which allowed for some moonlight to stream in, but it was still very dark.

"Should we go back and get a light?"

He chuckled quietly beneath his breath.

"I doona need it to find my way around this castle, and we willna need it once we get where I'm taking ye."

At the end of the hallway, we reached a door, and Raudrich released my hand as he opened it and stepped inside. I followed after him.

It was a bedchamber I'd yet to see, and this one was even larger and nicer than Raudrich's.

"I thought you said your bedchamber was the nicest."

"'Tis the nicest among The Eight. I doona include Nicol's room for this castle truly belongs to him. 'Tis only fitting that he should have the fairest room."

This bedchamber was a corner room and was unlike any room I'd seen in any castle I'd ever been in. The two outside walls were solid glass. They filled the room with a blue cast of moonlight that made it easy to see.

"Nicol had us spell these walls for him shortly after he gathered us here under his command. He is terrified of the darkness, though that is only a small reason why he sleeps during the day."

I'd thought earlier that it was odd that I'd not seen Nicol anywhere about until dinner. Now I knew why.

"What's the other reason?"

He reached for my arm and gently led me over to a large painted portrait that hung above Nicol's bed. It was the likeness of Nicol, though he was significantly younger in the painting. He stood behind a beautiful young woman. Her dark hair cascaded all the way down to her waist, and her eyes were so alarmingly black that I thought they might haunt me in my sleep.

"Who is that?"

Something about the portrait brought tears to my eyes. It had a heavy feeling to it, almost as if it might come alive if you looked away. It was creepy in a way that broke my heart.

"'Tis his wife, Freya."

"Is she…" it seemed slightly rude to ask such a blunt question, but it was the only assumption I could come to since I knew women weren't supposed to be inside the castle. "Is she dead?"

Raudrich shook his head. As I looked up into his eyes, I could see that he was saddened by this story, as well.

"'Tis far worse than that, lass. Nicol prays for her death, her true death, every day."

The insinuation that Freya was un-dead chilled me all over. Still staring at her portrait, I unconsciously took a step backwards and felt my back press against Raudrich's chest. He didn't step away from me. Instead, he placed his hands on my arms and began to rub me.

"The fright of it has chilled ye, aye? It does so to me every time I think of it, as well. Doona be scared. She canna harm ye. Would ye…" he hesitated and it only caused my fear to grow. "Would ye like to see her?"

"See her?" My voice was soft and unsteady as I twisted to look up at him. "Is she dead or not? If she's dead, I'm gonna be honest with you, I'd rather not."

He laughed and the warmth that radiated from his chest allowed me to relax just a little.

"Her body turned to dust long ago, but her spirit remains locked on this isle until the faerie below us either dies or releases Nicol and Freya from her grip."

"Huh?" He might as well have been speaking German.

"As I said, lass, 'twill be easier if ye allow me to show ye."

I was intrigued to be sure. It didn't mean that I wasn't also scared shitless.

"Don't move away from me, okay?"

In one swift motion, his hands moved from my arms and wrapped protectively around my front as he bent down and pressed his cheek flat against mine.

"I'll not go anywhere, lass."

Slowly, with his arms still wound around me, he moved me over so that we stood right in front of the large glass pane on the far side of the room. The view below was of a small garden that had been invisible to Marcus and me from the front of the castle.

Every plant and flower was withered and dead.

Nicol sat on a stone bench in the garden's center. The translucent figure of his wife—a ghost if I'd ever seen one—sat next to him.

CHAPTER 23

*a*ctually seeing a ghost was far less frightening than thinking about seeing one. As Raudrich and I looked down at Nicol and his wife, I felt no fear, only sadness.

"She's a ghost, then?"

"Not exactly." Raudrich kept his voice low. While I knew they couldn't hear us, I understood why he did. There was something intrusive about us staring down at their shared moment. "Ghosts rarely speak and they often repeat the same motions or move down the same paths over and over again. Freya is still who she was while living. She has thoughts and feelings and expresses them freely."

"But she's trapped there?" It was perhaps the most horrifying fate I could think of.

His voice was sad and reluctant.

"Aye. As I said, her fate is worse than death. If Nicol ever lives to see the day that she is released from this hell and she is able to once and for all truly die, he shall rejoice in it. We all will.

"During the day, she simply doesna exist, but each night she appears in her garden, cursed to see the man she loves but unable to feel his touch on her skin, doomed to never feel warmth again or to travel past the outskirts of her long-since wilted prison."

"Who would do that to her? Who would do that to anyone?"

I could think of no one I hated so much that I would wish them such a fate. No wonder Nicol looked so weary and sad. To spend his nights haunted by the love of his life, unable to help or save her, and to spend his days sleeping like a nocturnal animal—his existence had to be just as painful as her death.

"Are ye familiar with the fae, lass?"

I shook my head and had to keep from shivering at the way my cheek felt brushing back and forth against his stubble. It was dangerous for me to be this close to him. All I wanted to do was face him and repeat what I'd done to him last night.

"Only vaguely—a story here and there, perhaps. It's not something anyone really believes in or speaks of in America."

"Here." He released his hold on me and I immediately felt cold from the space that now lay between us. He moved toward Nicol's bed and quickly pulled a blanket off the top before sinking to the ground in front of the window. Gently he spread his legs out in front of him and motioned to the space in between. "Sit down, Laurel. Ye can lean against me while I tell ye the story. Ye are shivering where ye stand. I'll keep ye warm."

There was something mischievous in his voice. I kind of liked it. Smiling knowingly at him, I joined him on the floor. I sighed as I leaned back into his chest, and he draped the blanket over us. Once we were situated, he returned his arms to their place around my waist.

It was an intimate position for two strangers, but somehow I knew that our unacknowledged memories of the night before had us both feeling more comfortable around one another than we would have under normal circumstances. Sitting in his arms now, I felt rather silly for having denied any contact with him so ardently early in the day.

"Now, lass. Are ye ready to hear the true tale? Then, once I'm done ye can tell me just how right or wrong history has written it."

"Deal. I'm ready."

"This Isle has not always been known as The Isle of The Eight. Twenty years ago, 'twas The Isle of Whispers, and this castle was known as Murray Castle after Nicol's family and ancestors. He is one in a long line of Murray's that have tended to the people of this isle. For centuries, this land knew peace. When he was only five and thirty, his life became something other than his own.

"Ye see, fae are often spoken of in folktales as ways to frighten children into behaving as ye wish them to. But in truth, sightings of them and interactions with them are far less common than Scottish grannies throughout the country would have ye believe. Most doona truly believe they exist. Until my arrival on this isle as a child, I doona think I would've believed in them, either.

"Nicol was much the same. When one child from the village went missing, he thought it an accident, despite the insistence of the child's mother that a faerie had lured her son into the faerie land. Children often played too close to the water's edge or among rivers. He believed the child had been pulled away and drowned.

"But soon after, two more went missing, and their parents believed the same as the first. In an effort to stop the rising panic amongst the people of this village, Nicol went in search of the fae, and much to his misfortune, he found them."

I shivered as another chill swept through me. Acknowledging that magic time travel existed was one thing. Learning that ghosts and fairies existed was another. It seemed the world I'd spent most of my life living in was more sheltered than I realized.

"He found them here? On the isle?"

Raudrich nodded and pulled me in a little closer.

"Aye. All faeries are manipulative and selfish creatures. Ye canna trust a one of them, but Machara is worse than most. She yearned for a child—a half-human child—of her own. She captured the children of this village to lure Nicol away from the castle so she could strike a bargain with him: the safe return of the children she took for a night in his arms so she could have his child. It was a mistake he made in a moment and one that has placed a darkness over his entire life."

I twisted to look at Raudrich.

"She broke her bargain?"

"'Tis the way of faeries. They only keep their word to a degree. Machara returned the children, but they were not as they were. When they returned to their parents' doorsteps, they were older than their parents. For time doesna work the same in the land of the fae, and ye never know just how it shall ruin ye. Some men return to find they've stayed the same, but hundreds of years have passed. For the stolen children of this isle, their childhood was taken from them in the week they were gone."

"Oh, my God. Their poor parents."

"Aye. Many families fled here in response. They feared the same fate for their own children, and Nicol couldna blame them."

It was one of the saddest stories I'd ever heard, but it still didn't explain Freya's fate.

"And where does Freya come in?"

"Freya wouldna enter Nicol's life for another five years. Ye see, Machara loved the child she had with Nicol, and each year she would return to lie with him again. There are many tales of faerie lying with mortal men, but more often than not, 'tis the mortal that would be ruined with unquenchable lust and yearning for what they wished they could have but couldna—the love of the fae who used them.

"As with most things, Machara was different. She has never

followed the patterns of most fae. Nicol stayed indifferent to her, and slowly over the years as Machara bore more of his children—children he's never seen nor loved—she fell in love with him.

"Despite his annual obligations to Machara, Nicol believed himself a free man. During a short journey off the isle, he met and fell in love with Freya. Unaware of the doom it would bring them both, he married her before returning home. When Machara learned of Nicol's new wife, she went mad with jealousy.

"She confessed her love to Nicol and promised to forgive his trespass if he sent Freya away, but Nicol's love for Freya knew no bounds. He defied Machara and fled the isle with her.

"They spent five years away. They were the only happy years of Nicol's life. It was through his travels and his studies that he discovered a way to defeat Machara—it was how he came to form The Eight.

"Fae magic is stronger than that of any one witch or druid. Nicol learned that it would take many—the magic of eight—to cast the spell that would bind Machara for eternity. He and Freya traveled throughout Scotland gathering druid men young and old who were willing to pledge their loyalty and magic to him. I was among the first as were Harry, Maddock, Timothy, and Quinn. Ludo, Calder, and Paton joined us later after three of the original eight passed away.

"We practiced the spell for months before returning with him to the isle, for we all knew the spell would have to be cast almost immediately if we were to avoid Machara's wrath. We all urged him to leave Freya on the mainland until Machara was safely bound in her cell below the castle, but he couldna bear to leave her. He regrets that decision every single day."

I could no longer peel my eyes away from Nicol and Freya down below us. Their story was unlike anything I'd ever heard in my life.

"So what happened when you got here?"

"Machara saw us coming and awaited on the front steps of the castle, the lifeless bodies of each child she bore with Nicol laid out beside her. She hoped their death would riddle Nicol with guilt for abandoning her, but the children were inhuman things, beings he'd never known nor wanted. He felt nothing save relief that they'd not grow up to turn into beings as evil as their mother.

"His lack of emotion sent Machara into a rage, giving us just enough time to cast the spell as she lost her mind in a fit of screams and roars unlike anything I'd ever seen in my life. The spell worked, but not before Machara had time to do one last act of violence upon Nicol's life. She killed Freya by running her through with the sword she drew from Nicol's sheath. Just as Freya breathed her last breath, Machara cursed her to endure the state she is in now. It was the last thing Machara was able to do before our spell was finished and bound."

Raudrich drew in a sad, deep breath. It was clear that even telling the story exhausted him.

"For the past twenty years, Machara has remained locked away deep below this castle. As long as there are eight druids with their magic bound here, she canna escape. 'Tis why it is so urgent that we find another to replace Timothy, and why it is even more distressing that Calder has left us. Our magic is stretched until Timothy is replaced. If Calder finds a way to sever his tie with this isle, Machara may find the strength to break free."

Just as Raudrich finished his story, the sound of laughter, dark and sinister, traveled up through the floor beneath us.

"'Tis her, lass. 'Tis her dungeon that I meant when I said I must take ye somewhere ye willna wish to go. If ye want to know the truth of all of it, 'tis time for ye to meet Machara."

CHAPTER 24

*C*alder had been right about the smell in the storage room. I knew it the moment Raudrich opened the secret passageway in Nicol's room and we stepped into the dimly lit stairwell. It hadn't been the smell of rotten food. It was the smell of very angry faerie.

Lit candles lined the steps downward, but they cast an otherworldly green glow that should've been impossible through normal fire.

"Best ye breathe it in, lass. Ye will grow accustomed to it sooner that way. While I know 'tis foul, it willna harm ye."

I could scarcely bring my feet to move. Terror gripped at my every limb. I couldn't see her, and despite the fact that she was no longer laughing, I could feel her hatred in every nerve ending in my body. I grabbed at Raudrich as he stepped away and down one step.

"Wait. Raudrich, I don't think this is a good idea. She doesn't like women here, right? That's what Calder told Harry when he invited Marcus and me inside. Won't her seeing me make her even angrier?"

Raudrich's gaze was sympathetic as he turned toward me, but I could tell by the firm set of his feet that he had no intention of returning to Nicol's room.

"I should've been honest with ye, lass. I doona only wish to bring ye down here so ye might believe me. There is another reason, as well."

"Which is?"

He leaned in to whisper into my ear so quietly, even I had to strain to hear him.

"There is a reason Machara doesna wish for another woman to enter Nicol's home. Even in her anger, even in her rage, she pines for him still. She knows he can no longer touch Freya, no longer hold her and make love to her, so Freya is no longer a threat to her. But another woman, one that is still alive, just might be. If we can convince Machara that ye are not Nicol's and never shall be, perhaps we can prevent her from trying to harm ye while ye are here."

Even as frightened as I was, it hadn't occurred to me that she could actually cause me any real harm.

"Can she do that? Doesn't your magic keep her from doing harm to anyone?"

He took a deep breath. It did nothing to ease my worry.

"Until this morning, I would've said no. I would've been certain that she couldna do anything from her cell, but everything is different now that The Eight is no longer complete." He hesitated and looked regretful. "Lass, Maddock told me what happened today with Calder. While I'll make no excuses for what he said, he was right that the odor ye smelled was not from food."

I interrupted him. I didn't want to think on that moment a second longer.

"I know. The smell down here is the same."

He nodded. "Aye, and 'tis the first time such an incident has occurred. It means that her power has strengthened, and there is no way for us to know just how much."

I suddenly felt very willing to go along with whatever Raudrich needed me to do. I had no desire to be the target of an evil faerie's ill will.

"So how do we convince her that I have no interest in Nicol?"

He smiled. By the glint in his eye, I knew what he would say even before he said it.

"By convincing her ye belong to another."

---

*I*t was a rotten thing to put the lass through, but it truly was the only thing he could think of to keep her safe, and he was determined to do anything to do just that.

"Stay behind me, lass."

He knew it was an unnecessary directive. Laurel was plastered against him, and he knew she was doing everything she could to keep from shaking all over.

He'd not seen Machara in years, but the moment he lay eyes on her, all his hatred for her came rushing back.

She slinked toward the front of her cell, her silver hair dragging on the floor behind her, her long nails drumming against the rail as she smiled at him.

"Yer absence was good for me, Raudrich. 'Tis been more than a decade since I have felt this strong."

"Enjoy yer strength while ye can, Machara, for it willna last long. Timothy's body was weak for years before he died. The next druid will be stronger and with it, so will his magic."

She laughed, and the sound of it caused the hairs on his arms to rise.

"We shall see. Let me see the bitch behind ye, Raudrich. Let me see the whore that has come to try and seduce Nicol."

He'd known Machara would try to rile him up. He couldn't allow himself to give in to the anger he felt at hearing Laurel referred to in such a way. He needed his composure to keep his powers in check. It was even more important, with Laurel down here, that he not allow Machara to weaken him through rage.

"She is no threat to yer love for him, Machara. 'Tis why I thought ye should meet her."

Stepping away from the bars of her cell, Raudrich watched as Machara crossed her arms.

Carefully, he stepped away to clear the path between Laurel and Machara. He'd expected Laurel to hesitate, but she did no such thing. The strength in her steps shocked him. She didn't hesitate, didn't shake. She stepped up beside him, looked straight into Machara's eyes, and spoke. "I'm Laurel. I wish I could say that it's nice to meet you."

Machara gave one short chuckle as her sinister smile grew even wider.

"Ah, I see Raudrich has already tried to poison ye against me. If only we lassies could have spoken first, I doubt ye would have such an ill opinion of me. These men have never been able to understand me, but ye, I think could, if given the chance."

Raudrich could've laughed at the blasé expression on Laurel's face as she paused and pursed her lips. She cocked her head to the side in contemplation, but she knew better than to do anything that might anger Machara.

"I doubt that very much."

"So, tell me, whore, why are ye here? Do ye mean to take my Nicol from me?"

Raudrich watched the exchange with great anticipation. Everything was up to Laurel. How she decided to speak, what she decided to do next, would determine whether or not she was safe inside this castle.

"No. I may not like you, but I am not that sort of woman.

Raudrich watched as Machara's expression softened just the littlest bit, and hope rose within him.

"Who does yer heart belong to then? If it is still yer own, then ye are a threat, for a heart untethered is bound to fall for my Nicol."

Machara was crazy, but Raudrich's heart pounded in his chest as he awaited Laurel's answer. He hoped Laurel understood just how important it was that she give Machara a convincing answer. He hoped the lass was capable of being a better liar now than she had been this morning when trying to convince him that they'd not touched in his bed last night.

Laurel reached for him. Raudrich let out an uneasy breath as he stepped toward her and she wrapped her arm around his waist.

"My heart belongs to Raudrich, Machara. I give you my word as one woman in love to another. I shall never lay a hand on Nicol. My heart is already taken and always shall be."

If he wasn't so worried for Machara's reaction, Raudrich would've swooned at her words. It was convincing even to him.

Machara stayed silent for a long moment as she looked back and forth between them. As she did so, Laurel leaned into him even more, pressing her head into him as her hand came up to gently rub his chest.

When Machara did speak, there was humor in her tone.

"Kiss him, lass. Ye can always tell by the way someone kisses another what precisely is in her heart. Convince me that ye love him. If ye doona succeed, I suggest ye start fearing for yer life. For bound by magic or not, I have ways of ensuring that ye willna be long for this world. Kiss him like yer life depends on it, because trust me, young whore, it does."

Laurel's eyes pleaded with him to cooperate as she turned and reached up toward him. When her lips touched his, he crushed her against him, and together they danced for the damned faerie's pleasure and while he couldn't speak for Laurel, most assuredly his own, as well.

CHAPTER 25

*W*hile fear initiated our performance, I wasn't altogether sure it sustained it. The passion with which Raudrich pulled me against him—the heat and the weight of how he pushed me against the back wall of the dungeon—felt very real. And my response to him was no put-on. It was chemical, completely involuntary. I moaned against his lips as his tongue sought entry into my mouth. As his hands roamed down the side of my body and he backed me into the stones behind us, his lips moved to my neck. I let out a shaky breath in his ear that caused him to growl.

He pressed himself into my stomach, and I could feel how hard and ready he was. It was a familiar sensation, one I remembered all too well from only the night before. His hand cupped at my breast and I closed my eyes from the pleasure of it. I was losing myself— quickly forgetting about the evil faerie standing only a few short feet from us.

Then she spoke, and the reality of our surroundings crashed down on both of us as we awkwardly pulled away, both breathless and weak as Raudrich turned from me to look at her.

"I'll not waste my energy trying to harm ye, lass. Ye are not a threat. If ye are not in love with Raudrich now, ye are well on yer way to being so. My efforts would be better suited to trying to fight my way out of here while The Eight dwindle in number and power."

"Try as ye might, Machara, ye willna succeed as ye hope."

Raudrich's voice was deep and pained. He was still struggling to gain his composure. His response to me had been no performance. I was sure of it.

"Nothing stays buried forever, lad. Each and every one of ye should know that by now. One day I will be free of this cell. When that day comes, ye each shall suffer a fate far worse than Freya's."

Raudrich's left hand clenched at his side. I could see that he was growing angry.

Eager to be away from the smell and the terrifying gaze of such evil, I reached for his arm.

"Let's go. I don't think there's any need for either of us to say anything more."

Without a word, he took my hand and we turned to leave.

I knew I would hear her laughter in my sleep.

"*L*ass..."

Raudrich waited until we were far away from Machara—until we stood in the hallway outside his bedchamber—to say a word.

The hallways were dark, the castle quiet, and as he stopped and turned to look at me, all I could hear was his breathing, still ragged and strained.

"Yes?"

My voice shook as I answered him. The energy that passed between us as we stood facing one another, our chests nearly touching with each intake of uneven breath, was palpable in its heat and need. I'd never been so turned on in my life. I'd never been so confused.

This wasn't like me. I didn't do this. I wasn't the sort of person that got swept away with anything. I didn't know this man. How, then, could he make me feel so much?

I felt safe, yet scared—curious, but cautious. I wanted to throw my arms around him. I also wanted to run away as quickly as I could. Too many things stirred inside me as we stood in the darkness and silence together. It couldn't have been more than a few seconds, but the span of time between my breathless 'yes' and his answer felt like an eternity.

"Ye lied to me before. Why?"

It was hardly what I expected him to say, and with my thoughts clouded by his closeness, I couldn't recall what he might mean.

"Lie? When did I lie to you?"

He took one step closer and I felt my back bump into the wall behind me. I liked being pinned by him. I liked knowing that I couldn't avoid whatever he might do or say next. It was nerve-wracking in the sexiest way.

He leaned in and whispered in my ear. My whole body shivered as his breath wafted across the exposed skin of my neck. I closed my eyes and leaned back into the wall as he spoke.

"When I apologized for touching ye, ye said that I dinna do so. I know that I did, lass. Why did ye lie?"

"How do you know I was lying? Even if you think you touched me, perhaps it was only a dream."

I enjoyed this dance between us—his gentle prying, my pointless denial—it only served to increase the tension between us. It was so unlike me, but oh, so much fun.

"Because, lass…"

I gasped as he leaned in and cupped my breast in the small

hesitation between his words. My breast filled his hands and he groaned.

"Machara's dungeon was not the first time I've held this breast in my hand. I knew how ye felt in my arms before this night. My body remembers it clearly." He removed his hand and stepped away. "I'll ask ye once more. Why did ye lie?"

I reached out and placed both hands lightly on his chest. I wasn't ready for this closeness between us to end. I sighed as I prepared to come clean.

"I was embarrassed, Raudrich. You didn't touch me. I...I turned toward you in the night. You didn't pull me into your arms. I placed myself on your chest. I touched you. I rubbed against you with my leg. It wasn't your fault. None of it was. In my defense, I did believe I was dreaming, but when I woke and realized what I'd done, I was embarrassed."

I couldn't see his smile, but I could feel it in the darkness. He raised his hands and gently cupped my face.

"Embarrassed? Why?"

"I think because I enjoyed it so much. If it was a dream, I was safe in it. Once I knew it was real, I felt embarrassed that I wasn't really the woman I was in my dream—the woman who believed someone like you would want to hold me in such a way."

Only upon saying the words out loud, did I realize the truth in them. It wasn't my actions I was embarrassed by. It wasn't guilt at having touched him while he slept.

It was knowing that for me to act in such a way while I slept, my subconscious self must've believed I was desirable enough that there was no threat of rejection in my actions.

I wanted to be that person so very much. But—as many things seemed to be showing me since arriving in this time—my old self-conscious wounds weren't as healed as I thought.

I wasn't that confident go-and-get-what-you-want-woman that

had rolled over in my sleep and plastered herself against Raudrich as if she were doing him a favor. I was the woman that suspected every man's kind word held a motive. I was the woman that disbelieved every compliment—the woman that pulled away the moment a man got close because I couldn't see how they could possibly be genuine. Why on earth would they want me?

I was the woman that could play confident really well, that could sometimes even convince my mind that I was the confident woman I so desperately wanted to be. But deep inside, in my core, I was still that woman who didn't love herself enough to truly believe that anyone else could love her back.

When I'd woken in Raudrich's arms to find that my dream was real, it had broken my heart. For in real life, no longer free from all my self-loathing talk, all I could think was how much he wouldn't have wanted me if he had known I was there.

CHAPTER 26

*G*od, how he wanted her. He wanted her so badly it stunned him, too badly for him to do as he wished. She wanted him, too. He knew that if he kissed her, they would end up spending the night together. It would be the worst thing he could possibly do for her.

Her admission had made her too vulnerable. If he made love to her now, she would forever wonder if he'd done so out of pity or want. Marcus had been right. This lass, intoxicating as she was, didn't know how to play this game. He knew it all too well. He had an unfair advantage over her. He was older than her and no longer unsure of the man he was or what he wanted. He would wait until the game could be fair. He very much suspected that once she learned to let go and learned to embrace who she really was—once she learned to wield the power she already possessed—the wait would be worth it.

He would have to take things slowly with her. He would have to get to know her mind before he could know her soul, and he would need to know her soul before he allowed himself to taste of her body.

Laurel's fears weren't unusual. He'd known many women in his life that shared such insecurities. What women rarely could see was that men were often riddled even more with such worries.

She'd not known good men as a child, he was almost certain of it. For lassies surrounded by the best sort of men while still children grow up knowing just how lovely and special they are. Too many fathers discount the role they play in their daughter's lives—mayhap an even more important one than that of their sons. Raudrich knew that if he were ever lucky enough to be blessed with a daughter, he would make certain she knew that it was she and not the men she might know now and throughout her life that had the power to rule the world.

Perhaps, Laurel's time here would show her what good men could be—not that Calder's ignorant and cruel words had helped the situation. He would see to it that the rest of The Eight began to show her the best time of her life. It wouldn't take her long. Just a simple shift in her thinking could unleash her from the cage she kept herself in.

He looked down at Laurel as he held her face in his hands and gently bent to kiss her cheek.

"Lass, I do want to hold ye. I want to do so much more than that, but this night is not meant for us. 'Tis already the wee hours of the morning and ye are nearly asleep on yer feet. Go inside before I talk myself out of showing such restraint. Once ye close the door, I shall spell a lock for ye."

"I am rather tired."

Turning, she opened the door to his room and entered, but he couldn't keep from saying one last thing to her before she closed the door to him.

"Laurel, lass, I believe Morna lied to ye. I doona believe she brought ye here so ye could write a book."

Most nights, they lit their fires by hand so as to reserve their magic, but he didn't trust himself to step inside his bedchamber with her. With a quick flick of his wrist, he brought his room to light and his knees grew weak at the glint in her eye as she leaned into the doorway.

"Oh, yeah? Why do you think she brought me here then?"

"To heal what is broken inside ye and mayhap to find the love ye are so resistant to."

Laurel's brows pulled together and her tone was defiant when she spoke. "I'm not broken, Raudrich."

He wouldn't follow down the road she wished to lead him. He could sense it was one of the ways she so often pushed people away.

"Ye know that is not what I said, lass. Every one of us have broken pieces inside us, but we alone are the only ones that can heal them. Until we do, we canna become the people we are meant to be."

"And you've healed all your broken pieces, have you?"

"'Tis work that never ends, lass, but I shall never stop working to heal whatever may fracture inside me. Growing up here makes one less patient with the pain we cause ourselves. Not when ye know that pain could be brought on by another at any time—pain that ye canna control."

Laurel's eyes were sad and thoughtful as she gently sighed and closed the door between them.

CHAPTER 27

I fell asleep quickly after Raudrich left me. My mind was too full from all I'd seen that night, my body too alive from Raudrich's touch to process all of the things that were running through my mind. Instead, the moment my head hit the pillow, I was out, left to work through all of my thoughts as I slept.

I dreamed of Kate. She sat at the end of the bed and spoke to me as if she knew all that had happened—almost as if she were actually here.

"It's funny, isn't it? How I can tell you the same thing a hundred times and you won't hear it, but the minute you meet a man who calls you on your crap, you can actually see the problem."

Sitting cross-legged across from her, I answered.

"What crap? He didn't call me on any crap."

In my dream, Kate was whole again, unmarred from injury. She crossed her arms and lifted her brows at me. "Oh, really? How exactly did you read that then?"

I'd not had time to read into it at all. I was still processing Nicol and Freya's story, still reeling from the interaction with the wicked-scary faerie. By the time we'd gotten to Raudrich's room, I was so turned on, that all I'd been able to think was that I needed to get myself in the bedroom quickly or I was going to rip all of his clothes off.

Then came the whammy of my confession and all of the feelings I realized I didn't even know I was feeling until they came crashing down on me. My mind was too full and weary to read anything into Raudrich's last few words to me.

"I…" I hesitated and shrugged. "I don't know."

Kate shook her head and leaned in close.

"Well, then, let me tell you what he was not actually saying but definitely, totally meant."

I leaned back into the grand, carved headboard and settled in.

"By all means, Kate. Please do."

"That was a man who wants you, Laurel. But unlike most of the men you date, he's not going to let you chew him up and spit him out the moment you get scared or start to doubt your worth or feel a little self-conscious. He can see that you're not ready for him. You're not ready for something that's real, and he's not going to waste his time on anything but that."

There was no doubt my sister was wise, but all this seemed beyond her limited-insight into my complicated psyche.

"So what if I'm not ready? Everybody grows in their own time, Kate. It's just not time for me yet."

Kate held up one finger as if she were getting ready to list off a multitude of points.

"First correction: People rarely grow without trying. Change requires effort and you've been at a standstill for quite some time."

As I opened my mouth to argue, she threw up a second finger.

"Second: Don't be stupid, Laurel. Morna could've sent Marcus back here on his own. If she really cared about your writing inspiration, sending you the book and having us stumble across the documentary would've been more than enough. If it wasn't time for something to change in your life, she wouldn't have sent you back here."

"But…"

"No." She held up finger number three. "Three: Even if you don't feel ready, I suggest you get that way real quick. Do you really think that men like Raudrich come around every day? You've been on enough dates lately. You know that they don't. He read you like an open book, Laurel. He was able to get right to the bottom of your issues after spending three hours with you. Issues that you've become an expert on burying."

I knew she was right. I just didn't know what to do about it. I didn't know how to change. I didn't know how to start trying again.

"Okay, Kate, I get it. Something's got to give, but how? What do I do?"

She shrugged and I frowned. I didn't want her to give me some look inside bullshit, I wanted direction. I needed to know how to make a shift.

"Laurel, I'm no expert either, but just try doing things differently. Don't fall into the same traps you usually do with men. If Raudrich tells you something, believe him. You can see that he likes you. Don't question it so much. Stop doubting how beautiful you are. How about this?"

She hesitated and lifted herself to her knees. She looked beyond excited at whatever revelation had just come to her.

"How do you write your characters, Laurel? They're confident and sassy. They do what they like and say what they want. They don't rail against their own happiness because they believe that they are deserving of it, right? They're different from you, but if you were really honest with yourself, I think you'd find that they're all a part of you, too. I have a theory. I think those characters, those heroines in your stories, they're really just all of the parts of you that you keep locked away. How about, just for a little while, just while you're here, you let them out to play for a bit. Pretend you're them. It may just show you who you really are."

It was an interesting thought, but before I could say so, Kate disappeared. I blinked once and opened my eyes to find that Morna now occupied the same spot Kate had just vanished from.

"I thought perhaps ye might be more open to hearing from Kate since I suspect ye and Marcus are still a wee bit upset with me."

I frowned. Seeing Kate made me miss her. After so many months being around her day and night, I wasn't accustomed to being away from her.

"So all of that was really you? Why am I not surprised? Raudrich was right then? You did lie to me?"

Morna nodded and smiled unapologetically. "Aye, lass. I wasna sure if ye would embark upon the travel back if I told ye the truth. Though, at the time, I dinna know that I was going to have to spell ye back against yer will. I regret how angry Marcus is with me."

I shrugged. I couldn't find it in me to be angry with her. Evil faerie and cursed castle aside, I was enjoying myself. I'd lived more in the last three days than in the past three years.

"Marcus is trying to make the best of it. Although, I have a feeling that after what I tell him tomorrow, that's going to be more difficult for him to do."

Morna sighed and I could see that I was right.

"Aye, he willna take the news well. Not for some time, I expect. Ye must allow him to work through it in his own way. Doona take it personally if he pushes ye away."

That didn't worry me in the least. Marcus wasn't like me. He didn't push people away. He talked things out. He was more of a grown-up than I imagined I would ever be. He wouldn't do to me what I'd done to him after our last trip to Scotland.

"Marcus isn't like that. He'll be upset, but not with me."

"Whatever ye say, lass. I must go now. 'Tis time for ye to wake. Marcus is standing outside yer door. 'Tis time for ye to tell him the truth."

With my next breath, my eyes opened.

Why were my dreams in this castle so flipping weird?

CHAPTER 28

"*L*aurel, are you up? If not, wake up and let me in before everybody else wakes up. I am freaking out. The door's bolted. Let me in."

Slipping back into my dress—I'd dared to sleep naked again—I walked over to the door and unlatched the bolt Raudrich had magically placed there.

"What is it? What's wrong?"

He was covered in sweat.

"Shut the door. I don't want to risk anyone hearing me."

Once the door was shut, he began to pace back and forth across the length of the room.

"Marcus, what happened?"

"I don't know what happened, Laurel. I woke up early and it was freezing in my room. I was laying there with every cover in the room wrapped around me trying to decide if it was worth the effort of uncovering myself to walk across the room and light a fire. Then, out of nowhere, the fire just lit itself."

"It lit itself?"

He nodded. "Yes. And that's not all. I lay there trying to justify

159

it, right? Because otherwise I worried I would go running from this castle screaming. So, I tried to calm myself down by thinking things like '*maybe they have the fires set on some sort of timer*,' or '*maybe there was still a bit of lit kindling in the bottom from before bed and it sparked just right.*' But then..." he paused and placed his palm against his forehead as if he still couldn't believe it. "I lay there and began to think, '*hmmm...I wonder what time it actually is? I wonder if it's still dark out?*' And then, the curtains covering each of the windows on either side of the bed just opened. On their own, Laurel."

He stopped pacing and moved to stand right in front of me.

"Laurel, this castle, these men, they're in my head. They're listening to my thoughts. Someone is doing something to me. I don't like it. I don't like it one bit."

I knew what it was. It wasn't remotely what he thought, and I had no idea how to tell him.

"Marcus, sit down. You look like you've just run five miles."

"I feel like it. My heart is beating fast enough."

I patted the bed and waited until he took a deep breath and moved to join me.

"How are you so calm, Laurel? You don't look surprised at all."

"If you'd seen what I saw last night, you wouldn't be either."

And so it began. I told him everything. I told him where Raudrich had taken me and all about what had happened to Nicol and Freya. I told him about Machara's cell down below the castle and what had happened when Raudrich took me down to see her. I told him about the way Raudrich had held me in his arms while he told me Nicol's story, and the way I felt when I kissed him in front of Machara. I took my time describing the entire night. I was in no hurry to get to the end of the story—to the part where I would have to tell him what he was.

By the time I finished, Marcus' breathing had returned to normal and he appeared much calmer than before.

"He likes you, you know? I could tell he did at dinner last night."

I nodded. I was going to try and take dream-Kate's advice. I wouldn't question what I felt to be true.

"I know, but we don't need to talk about me and Raudrich right now. There's something I have to tell you."

Marcus chuckled, and I sincerely hoped it wouldn't be the last time he would laugh for the foreseeable future.

"Even more happened last night? Geez, Laurel, that was enough to fill up a week."

I could sense it then—as the words formed in my mind—just how much this would hurt him. The news would be bad enough, but once he learned that I'd suspected this even before Morna sent us back here and didn't tell him…I wasn't sure if he would ever be able to forgive me.

"Marcus, this doesn't have to do with last night. This has to do with you. Something happened before we left for Scotland. Something I now know, I really should've told you about before now. I just…" I started to ramble the way I always did when nervous. "If it turned out to be nothing—which I was pretty sure it would—I didn't want to worry you for no reason. But Marcus, it wasn't nothing. It was a really, really big something and I'm so sorry."

He looked confused as I started to cry.

"Laurel, calm down. It can't possibly be as bad as all that. Just tell me."

"I know I told you about the documentary and the book. Those really are the reasons I wanted to come here. Although, as we both know now, they were what Morna used to prep me for where she was sending us."

Marcus reached for my hands and gently rubbed his thumb back and forth across my knuckles. It pained me more than he could know that he was trying to comfort me as I was trying to figure out how to deliver news to him that would change his life forever.

"I know all that, Laurel."

"I know. But there's something I left out. Something I didn't tell you about the book that I found."

He didn't look worried.

"Okay…what didn't you tell me?"

"You're going to hate me, Marcus."

He leaned forward and kissed my forehead. It made my heart ache.

"I could never hate you."

I took a deep breath and braced myself.

"There was a portrait in the book. A portrait of The Eight. You were in the portrait."

He didn't seem to understand.

"Well, we are here now, aren't we? Maybe the portrait is painted while we're here."

"No, you weren't next to The Eight. You were *one* of the The Eight."

I took another deep, shaky breath as I watched realization set it.

"I don't think they're inside your head, Marcus. I think your own powers are starting to come to the surface. I think you're destined to be one of The Eight."

CHAPTER 29

The sudden burst of magic throughout the castle startled him from his sleep. The magic of The Eight was connected—each could feel when another used their powers. This magic was different. It belonged to another.

Raudrich rose from bed quickly. As he stepped outside of Calder's room, he could hear the others rousing. Such a change in the energy of the castle wouldn't go unnoticed by any of them.

Ludo, whose room lay next to Calder's, joined him in the hallway.

"What in the name of Brighid was that? It couldna have been Calder, aye? We would've known if it were him."

It wasn't Calder. If Calder had used his powers or tried to sever them from The Eight, it would've been recognizable. This magic was not.

"No, 'twas not Calder."

Quinn appeared at the end of the hallway, and together they moved to meet him.

"Has anyone seen to Machara? Could it be her?"

As if summoned, Nicol entered the castle doors from his place in the garden. While he possessed no powers of his own, he was linked to the castle and all within it. He could feel the use of magic just like the rest of them.

"I shall make certain she is still locked away. Gather everyone else. We must discern what has just happened."

As Raudrich watched Nicol run toward his bedchamber, he turned to look at Ludo and Quinn.

"I doona believe this is Machara's doing. 'Twas not the magic of the fae."

"I agree." Quinn's voice was sure and certain. "There was no malice in it, though it felt strong and somehow uncontrolled."

Raudrich racked his mind for an answer. In truth, there was only one possibility, even as shocking as it was.

"The magic came from within the castle, aye? We can all agree on that?"

Both men nodded in agreement.

"And we know that 'twas not one of us. There is only one other answer, lads. The magic came from one of our guests. Either Marcus is a druid or Laurel a witch."

Was it possible that he'd spent so much time with her and not seen it? Could she have hidden it from him so well?

He had to find out straight away.

Before either man could even respond to him, he took off toward his own bedchamber, calling after Ludo and Quinn as he left.

"Ye two round up the others. I shall go to Nicol to make certain all is well with Machara. Then, I shall collect Laurel and Marcus, and we will get to the bottom of this in the dining hall."

*T*here was no time to gauge Marcus' reaction. The moment I told him my suspicion, the door to the bedchamber flew open and Raudrich stepped inside.

His expression was surprised. If I didn't know any better, I would've said he looked wounded. He looked quickly between me and Marcus and then locked his gaze with mine. He didn't blink as he spoke.

"Is it ye, Laurel? If so, why dinna ye tell me? I trusted ye with everything ye wished to know about this castle without a second thought. It hurts me that ye dinna trust me enough to do the same."

Marcus was silent next to me and his own gaze was turned downward. I could see him wrestling with what I'd just told him. If not for his own experiences before waking me, he would've laughed at my suspicions, but the incident had been enough to make him wonder if it could be true, and he didn't have the slightest idea how to handle it, if it was.

I stood and walked the short distance to Raudrich and gently reached for his arm. He stepped away to prevent me from touching him.

"What are you talking about?"

"The magic, lass. Everyone in the castle felt it. Did Morna even send ye here, or did ye tell me that so I wouldna learn ye were a witch?"

I chuckled.

"Well, I sure didn't feel it. I'm not a witch, Raudrich. I didn't even know true magic existed until a few days ago."

He looked as if he meant to argue with me, but before he could do so, Marcus stood from his seat on the end of the bed.

"Neither did I, but apparently I possess it. It was me. Whatever happened, it was me."

Raudrich's expression softened at Marcus' tone. He could hear the weariness and confusion in it.

"Ye dinna know, did ye lad?"

Marcus shook his head. I tried to catch his gaze as he walked over to us, but he wouldn't look at me. A knot settled in my stomach. He was going to do exactly as Morna had predicted in my dream. He was going to push me away.

"Of course I didn't know."

"Has anything strange ever happened around ye before?"

"No."

Raudrich reached out and gently clasped Marcus on the shoulder.

"There is much we must discuss with ye. I know ye must have many questions and even more reservations. We are the only ones that can explain any of this to ye. Will ye come with me to the dining hall? The men are gathering there."

Nodding, Marcus stepped toward the doorway. When I reached out to touch his arm, he whirled on me.

"Don't touch me, Laurel and don't say a word. I know it was me that suggested we come back to Scotland, but I did that for you. I came here for you. And you suspected before we even left this might be my fate, and you didn't care enough about me to tell me that. If I'd known, I never would've come here. You took that from me, Laurel. You took away my choice. You've taken away my life. How can I possibly ever forgive you for that?"

One tear fell down his cheek, and with it, my heart broke completely.

Sobbing, I tried to reason with him.

"Marcus, I'm so sorry. I should've..."

He held up a hand to stop me.

"Don't. You're selfish, Laurel. So damned selfish. I'm done with you. If I'm going to be trapped here forever, I sure as hell don't want you here with me. Start looking for a way to get Morna to send you home. Until you find one, stay out of my sight."

He stormed away as I sobbed. Once Marcus was out of earshot, Raudrich pulled me into a hug.

"Lass, I think it best that ye stay away from the dining hall today. This shan't be easy on the lad, but with time he will see this for what 'tis—his destiny. He will make his peace with it, and when he does, he will see that ye are not the one to blame. I'll seek ye out later, lass."

I stood shaking in the doorway, tears running down my face, for hours.

I'd never felt more ashamed or alone.

CHAPTER 30

*S*ometime during the middle of the afternoon—long after I'd run out of tears—I began to hear lots of movement in the hallways and throughout the castle. Whatever they were doing, the men seemed to be in a hurry. While my curiosity was killing me, I knew better than to leave Raudrich's room. Marcus didn't want to see me. I wasn't particularly keen to see him either.

So, as the footsteps, hollering, and commotion continued, I knew I needed to find a way to occupy myself. Otherwise, I would lose my mind. First, I set out to light a fire, which to my everlasting surprise, I succeeded in doing. Second, I shamelessly rummaged around Raudrich's room and opened every chest until I found what I was looking for—parchment, ink well, and a quill.

There was only one person I wanted to talk to. One person that could make me feel a little less alone and hated.

It took me a bit of time to get used to the ink and the rough way the tip of the quill scraped against the thickness of the paper, but I was eventually able to write something legible.

Morna,

I'm going to trust that your word was true and try throwing this note into the fire. If so, send me something, some way that I can speak to my sister. I miss her and I'm really in need of a talk with her—a real one. Not some cloaked version of you that you send to me in my dreams.

Laurel

Tearing the parchment just below my small note, I folded it up and tossed it into the fire. All it did was burn. Frustrated, I moved to the windowsill and looked down into the steep slope of forest that cascaded down the hill surrounding the castle. As I stared across the landscape, there was a slight swooshing sound behind me. I turned to see a folded note fly out of the flames, totally untouched by fire, and land gently on the writing desk where I'd just been sitting,

I hurried over to the table, gently touched the note's edge to make certain it wasn't warm and tore it open.

Laurel,

I know that neither of you seem to believe me, but I do only lie when it is absolutely necessary, lass. If I told you that you could reach me this way, I meant it. Walk over to Raudrich's wardrobe and open the door. At the bottom you will find what you need, but for the love of God, lass, keep it hidden. It would never do for something so modern to be discovered in the time you're in.

It seemed like too much to hope for, but I stood and ran over to the wardrobe and nearly tore the handle from the door in my haste to see if it could possibly be true.

It was.

Right at the bottom lay a phone. Beaming, I picked it up and ran back over to the parchment to respond.

I suppose this doesn't actually need service to work, does it? Thank you.

It wasn't a serious question. I knew, of course, that the phone would need no towers or battery to work.

Morna's response was almost instantaneous.

Of course not. Laurel, this phone shall be the last gift I give you and the last time I'll respond to anything you may write, for I know where your questions will lead, and I can't help you with what must come next. History has cast the die over what shall happen with Machara and the men of this castle. In this case, it wouldn't do for me to interfere. There are too many lives destined to take part in this story, too many things that need to fall into place.

I know you must think this very hypocritical of me, and perhaps it is. From reading my own story, you know that I've changed history more than once, but this time, history doesn't need my meddling to work out well in the end. Remember that when it feels like your world is falling apart.

With love and hope, I leave you.

Morna

I stared at the note, reading it over and over again as I tried to process what she might mean. I had a sinking feeling that I already knew.

Despite her warning, I scribbled out another note and through it into the flames.

Does this mean that I'm stuck here? What about my family? What about Marcus' family? What about our lives back home?

I waited the rest of the day for her answer.

171

It never came.

And that in and of itself was answer enough.

I would never see Boston again.

---

*A*t first Raudrich believed it wasn't working. Perhaps, Marcus' magic was still too new. Mayhap, they would have to teach him to wield his new powers before its strength was potent enough for the spell to bind him to The Eight.

But then, slowly, as their chanting continued, Marcus' face distorted in pain as Machara's screeches rose up from her cell beneath them. The room shook around them as the binds took hold.

Marcus was now one of The Eight.

It should've been a relief to all of them, but as Raudrich looked into the eyes of his brethren, he knew the same worry weighed heavily on all of them.

Until Calder was found and his true motive for leaving known, they were no safer today than they'd been the day before.

CHAPTER 31

*J*t wasn't ideal, but it was the only agreement they could come to.

Marcus' magic was now bound, but it would take months for him to learn to harness the powers that were still his own. He would have to be trained as soon as possible.

Marcus wasn't the only pressing matter. Finding Calder was just as important.

So, after much discussion and many an argument, a plan was set.

All would leave the castle, save him. He would stay to keep an eye on Machara and to see that Laurel was safe. They couldn't risk Laurel leaving with the men who would go in search of Calder, and Marcus wouldn't hear of having her near him.

Even Nicol would leave with the other men—something he'd not done in over a decade.

Paton, Quinn, Ludo, and Marcus would leave for the Isle's furthest corner, far away from the castle where they would spend the following fortnight training The Eight's newest member and helping him to adjust to his new life among them. Such training couldn't be done near the castle grounds where Machara could listen in. She would only look for ways to exploit Marcus' weaknesses if they remained close to her.

The others—Harry, Maddock, and Nicol would leave for the Scottish mainland where they would begin to search and inquire into Calder's whereabouts. He couldn't have gotten far in the span of only a few days. Once they found him, they would hold him prisoner until Marcus' training was complete. Then as a group, they would decide what was to be done with him.

If his only trespass had been his thoughtless words about Laurel, forgiveness would've been the only possibility. They all knew just how easily Machara's power could strike fear into their hearts. Fear could make a fool of any man. What was less easily decided was whether his abandonment was enough to cast him out. If so, it would be a heartbreaking decision for them all.

"What should I do while the rest of ye are away? Is there some task undone, some measure I could take to further assure our safety that was neglected while I was gone?"

Raudrich felt rather useless standing there, watching every other man in the castle ready their horses for their journey. Not that he wished to leave. It was clear that someone must stay and tend to the castle, and there was no possibility of him allowing another man to stay here with Laurel alone.

Harry walked over and roughly punched his arm.

"Come now, Raudrich. We all know that even if I were to tell ye something ye could do, ye are unlikely to do it, not with Laurel about. Ye think of nothing else even when we are here. When we are away, it shall only be the two of ye—possibly for some time."

The anticipation of such extended time with her both delighted and filled him with dread. It was important that he tread carefully with the lass even if it was the last thing he wanted to do.

"Aye, I know. I shall be in need of a distraction."

"I'll not be the one to give ye one. Ye must know that every last one of us would gladly take yer place if we could. To have a lassie as lovely as Laurel, one that clearly likes ye, is a gift I'll not let ye waste. This life we lead here has denied each of us happiness that all men should know. If ye have a chance at finding love, lad, take it. Besides," Harry laughed and clasped his arm. "I know we give ye a hard time for leaving us these past two years, but we all know ye dinna have a choice. And I'd reckon ye worked far harder in those two years than the rest of us have in a decade. Think of this time here as a respite for ye. 'Tis likely we've some tough choices ahead, so find some joy in the days ahead while ye can."

If they did decide to remove Calder from The Eight, the decision would weigh on no one as much as Harry. Harry had been like a father to Calder for most of his life. It pained Raudrich to know how difficult all of this must be for him.

"I'm sorry, Harry. I know that all this with Calder has been difficult for ye."

Harry cleared his throat and looked to the ground.

"Aye, and I canna help but bear some responsibility for it. I've known for some time Calder was struggling. I should've paid him more mind. There is no true evil in Calder's heart. I've hope still that if we find him, his reason for this all will be clear. Doona give up on him yet."

Raudrich nodded. Even with the anger he had for Calder, it wasn't an easy thing to give up on family.

"I shan't. Safe travels, friend. May he be safe and well when ye find him."

Harry walked away from him and mounted his horse with ease as the rest of the men waved and took off toward the gate. He called back to him as he took his place at the tail end of the group.

"Enjoy yerself, Raudrich. Doona squander time that the rest of us would cherish. Farewell for now, my friend."

He waited until he could no longer see them before turning toward the castle.

He didn't care for Laurel's tears. The pain in her eyes as Marcus screamed at her had made him hurt all over.

If it was just to be the two of them there for weeks, he would see to it that her smile was returned to her as quickly as possible.

I didn't call Kate right away. I knew that before I spoke to her I needed to gather myself. I needed to reflect on how I felt about being stuck in this time for the rest of my life, and I needed to decide what I would tell her.

What surprised me more than anything was that the panic I expected to set in never did, neither did the heartbreak or fear. The truth was, I wasn't upset about staying here.

It wasn't that I was ignorant. I knew that with time, there would be many things I would miss. But deep down, if Marcus was destined to be here, then I knew I was destined to be here, too. We were family. Neither of us had ever functioned very well without the other. Boston just wouldn't suit me without him. And I knew—even as angry as he was with me now—seventeenth century Scotland wouldn't suit him without me, either.

There was only one person and one ornery cat that I would miss immeasurably—Kate and Mr. Crinkles. But for some reason I couldn't quite explain, Kate's distance didn't overwhelm me with pain. It didn't feel permanent, even though I knew it most likely was. At least, I would be able to speak to her. That was no small blessing.

I didn't hear Raudrich open the unbolted door. I was too busy turning Morna's magical phone over and over in my hands as I tried to decide how to tell Kate that I would never be returning home.

"Come, lass. Ye've been in this room for far too long today. How would ye like to venture out of this castle and meet some of the people of the village?"

As curious as I was to meet even more people from this time, it was the last thing I wanted to do tonight. My mind was much too occupied.

"It's all right, Raudrich. I don't want to run the risk of bumping into Marcus, and I'm exhausted anyway."

He laughed and came to crouch down in front of me as he placed his hands on my knees.

"From what, lass? Sitting by the fire all day? 'Tis not good for anyone to sit all day. And ye needn't worry about crossing paths with yer friend. He's gone."

I started and pulled back in my seat.

"Gone? What do you mean, he's gone?"

"I'll not lie to ye and tell ye he's pleased with any of this, but as we spoke with him and tested his powers, he couldna deny their existence. He agreed to join us. He became one of The Eight this afternoon. He's gone with half the men to train and learn how to use his magic. He willna be back for weeks."

Perhaps, I shouldn't have felt so relieved at Raudrich's news, but I was. Confrontation had never been my thing, and confrontation with those I loved most was definitely something I shied away from. With Marcus gone, I could move about freely without worrying about his angry glances, and I couldn't help but be glad about it.

"Oh. Well, that's good, I suppose. What's everyone else doing? There was so much noise earlier, but it's quiet now."

He smiled rather guiltily.

"They're gone as well, lass—on their way to the mainland to

search for Calder. 'Tis only ye and I," he hesitated, "and Machara and poor Freya in all of the castle. While I've much to worry over, I doona wish to do it this night."

He moved his hands from my knees and gathered my hands in his own.

"Do ye know how long it has been since I've had time without duty or obligation, Laurel? I havena had a day to myself in over two years. Please doona make me celebrate this time of freedom all on my own."

His excitement made him look much younger than he was—like the young boy inside him was finally getting a chance to peek out for the first time in ages. How could I possibly say no?

For the first time all day, I smiled.

"I…I look like a bit of a mess. I've been crying, and I've worn this same dress for days. It smells of horse."

"Not to worry about that, lass. I've laid out four of Freya's gowns for ye. They may be a wee bit short on ye, but no one shall notice that, I assure ye. I've also prepared a bath for ye in Marcus' room."

While I knew Freya had no real use for her dresses anymore, it still seemed rather intrusive for me to wear one of them.

"Is it okay for me to wear one of Freya's dresses? Do you think she would mind?"

He smiled and shook his head.

"No, lass. I asked her. With Nicol gone, I spent some time with her just as soon as the sun went down. I know she will be lonely without him. 'Twas she who suggested it."

What a strange life I was living—to be offered up dresses by a ghost.

"Okay, then. I'll um…I'll meet you downstairs when I'm ready."

I stood and walked toward the hallway when I heard him call after me.

"I canna wait, lass. I hope ye know how to dance. The people of this village havena seen me in years. I suspect they'll throw quite the party in the tavern for me."

I didn't—like, at all. I was far too excited to care.

CHAPTER 32

*R*audrich hadn't lied. While the tavern was nearly empty upon our arrival, it didn't take long for word to spread that Laird Peyton, as he was known here—I still didn't know why—was back. Before long, everyone in the village arrived. Raudrich was met with more greetings and hugs than I could count. Within a few minutes, he was pulled away from me.

I didn't mind. The people of the village were more than accommodating and I wasn't alone for a moment. As the hours went by, I danced, talked, and drank with nearly everyone in the village. By the time Raudrich came to collect me, I was dizzy from dancing, stuffed full of food, and had just enough ale in me to make my cheeks rosy and my tongue a little looser than normal. I was in a better humor than I'd been in ages.

I wished Marcus and Kate were here to see it. I wasn't sure either of them would recognize this version of me.

"There ye are. I promise ye 'twas not my intention to abandon ye here on yer own. I knew my arrival would be a festive occasion, but I dinna know just how many people would wish to speak with me. I am verra sorry, Laurel."

He stood next to me but leaned in close as he spoke.

I reached out and gave his arm a gentle squeeze as I smiled at him.

"It's okay. Really, it is. I had a great time."

He smiled back and surprised me by placing a protective hand on the lower part of my back.

"I can see that, lass, but do ye mind if we leave now? 'Twas ye I wished to spend my time with, and I havena seen ye at all."

"I don't mind at all. I don't think my feet could take any more dancing anyway."

He smiled and slowly laced his hand with mine. The gesture surprised me. I wouldn't have expected him to want to do anything that gave the impression that I was with him, not when Raudrich and I, while undeniably attracted to one another, were still no more than friendly acquaintances. What surprised me even more was that no one in the tavern seemed surprised in the least.

"Not even with me, lass? I spent the whole night watching ye, and I envied every man that held ye in his arms."

The admission sent an anticipatory thrill down my spine, but I waited until we stepped out into the cool Scottish air to answer him.

"I might have one more dance in me, but if you were watching, you know how bad I am at it. Everyone was so nice, but I know I stepped on every single one of my partners' toes."

The biggest full moon I'd ever seen hung in the sky, making it easy for us to see our way back to Raudrich's horse.

He helped me up first then deftly mounted the beast behind me. I was settled into him even more closely than I'd been on the way down to the village, and I didn't miss how easily he rested his hands on my thighs.

"Raudrich?"

"Hmm?" He leaned his chest into my back as he reached for the reigns. His face was pressed against my own, and I thought I felt his lips brush against my cheek for the briefest moment, but I couldn't say for sure.

"Why do they call you Laird Peyton?"

"Ah. I forget that ye still know so little about me, lass. Most of The Eight came from humble families, so they were free to use their true names when they pledged their loyalty to Nicol and this Isle. My family owns a large portion of Northern Scotland. My brother was laird there for many years. If it were ever to be known that I abandoned my familial clan and pledged my loyalty to another, it would've caused many problems for my brother when he was alive, so I took another name when I came here.

While we dinna know it at the time, 'twas good that I did so. When my brother and his wife were murdered, his land was passed to me. I became laird of Allen territory. 'Twas not truly mine by right, as I broke my vows to my familial clan long ago, but because I hid my true name, it allowed me to see my brother's people settled after his death and to take the time I needed to sign the land over to someone I knew to be trustworthy."

"I'm so sorry, Raudrich."

He sighed and straightened himself just a little.

"Thank ye. I dinna know my brother as well as I wish I had. Though, the loss of him was painful, all the same."

His tone made it clear it wasn't something he liked to speak about. I hurried to change the subject.

"I've realized something, Raudrich. I think it is time that I make my peace with being here. I don't think I'll ever be going home."

He was quiet a long moment. When he did speak, his voice was thoughtful.

"How do ye feel about that? There must be much that ye left behind. It canna be easy."

It was a short ride to the castle gates. I could already see them in front of us.

"Not the way I should feel about it, probably. I'll miss my sister dreadfully, but...I don't know. Would you believe me if I told you that even though I've only been here a few days, I feel as if I'm meant to be here? As if this time was meant to be my real home all along?"

Raudrich pulled on the horse's reigns as we reached the gate. He dismounted quickly and turned to offer me his hands. I allowed him to pull me off and into his arms. Our bodies rubbed against one another as he slowly set me to my feet. He didn't step away. He stood there with his hands on either side of my ribs as he looked down into my eyes.

"I told ye last night, lass. 'Tis not only this time I think yer meant for, but this verra castle, as well. I believe ye shall find yer heart here. Mayhap, the love ye've always wished for."Whether it was the tavern ale or my determination to be bold, I didn't know, but for once in my life, I allowed myself to say the exact thing that was on my mind.

"And you think you might be that love?"

He smiled and moved his right hand to the side of my face, cupping it gently as his thumb trailed back and forth across my cheek.

"I doona believe either of us can say that yet, but whomever captures yer heart shall be lucky to have it. If time shows us that I am that man, I shall wake up every blessed day grateful for it."

I was shaking again, and my cheeks were warm from more than just ale.

"Kiss me then, not because you're trying to save me from some jealous faerie, but simply because you want to."

"What makes ye think that I do want to kiss ye, lass?"

There was a test in his question. He wanted my certainty, none of the doubt I'd shown him the night before.

"Oh, you don't, huh?" I smiled at him so he'd know I wasn't

upset by his question. "I guess I'll just…" I brushed past him and started to walk away, but he quickly reached for my hand and spun me back toward him.

"There ye are, lass—a woman who doesna doubt what she does to a man. How long have ye kept her locked away?"

I answered honestly. "Forever, I think."

He leaned in until his lips were nearly touching my own.

"Please doona ever lock her away again. Allow me to show ye just how powerful she is."

His kiss was hungry and demanding as he pulled me against him. I reached for his hair as I leaned into him. I cried out into his mouth as he gently nipped at my lip.

"The distance to the castle shall seem like an eternity, lass. Best we get the horse to his stable before I doona have the strength to pull away from ye."

Just as he broke our kiss, the sound of horses approached and a very American voice spoke out through the darkness.

"Raudrich, I am going to freaking kill you. Do you know how long it's taken me to find you?"

CHAPTER 33

*R*audrich staggered away from Laurel, his arousal painful in its intensity. Thank God for the darkness. Without it, he would've been unable to shield it from view. Shaking his head, he tried to pull himself together and think clearly as the small group of riders approached. He'd been certain he would never see or hear from Sydney again. How could she possibly have found him? As the group of riders came into view, his confusion only grew.

Pinkie led the group, his wide smile and few teeth making him unmistakable even in the shaded darkness. Next to him rode Sydney —her voice and dark hair the giveaway. The other two riders, he couldn't yet see.

"Sydney, lass, what are ye doing here?" He looked over to Pinkie before his friend even had time to respond. "Pinkie? Do ye know Sydney?"

Pinkie spoke first, quickly dismounting before walking over to shake his hand.

"It seems yer sight has returned. Ach, I am glad of it, Raudrich. To answer yer question, aye, I know Sydney now, though I dinna a few days ago. I was halfway home when I stopped at a small inn and came across these three. When I heard the description of the man they were looking for, I knew 'twas ye. So, I offered them my assistance, for a price, o'course."

He nodded as he shook the man's hand.

"Naturally." He stepped away. He could feel Sydney's anger at a distance. "Excuse me, Pinkie, I believe I've some apologies to make."

"Aye, ye do. I dinna know lassies knew such language. I only thought wives got so angry at men, but she swears she doesna love ye in such a way."

Ignoring Pinkie, Raudrich hesitantly walked over to Sydney's horse and extended her his hand.

"Let me help ye."

She crossed her arms and shook her head.

"No, thank you. I've lived in this bloody time long enough to know how to get myself on and off a damn horse. Open the gate. I see no need to dismount before we actually get to the castle. When we do, though, you and I are having a nice, long talk. Alone. Do you understand?"

He would never say so, but it pleased him that Sydney was angry. It meant she was the true friend he knew her to be.

"Fine, lass, but who is that ye've brought with ye?"

Both riders brought their horses closer as he mentioned them.

"Silva?"

It couldn't be good that the lass who was meant to be tending to Allen territory was here.

"'Ello, Raudrich. Once Sydney is done with ye, 'tis I who needs to speak with ye. I'm not so pleased with ye, either."

He didn't recognize the man next to Silva, but the man spoke up as he looked at him.

"I've no need to speak with ye, so ye can relax yer mind a little.

Ye may not know me. It has been some time since we last met. I'm Griffith MacChristy."

Upon hearing his name, Raudrich could see the resemblance the boy bore to his brothers, but the lad was right. The last time he'd seen young Griffith, the lad had been little more than a boy. Now, he was a strapping beast of a man.

"Aye, I do know ye. Ye've grown."

He turned to unlock the gate.

"Come. All of ye. "'Tis too cold out for us to continue this outside."

He stood beside the gate allowing the others to ride inside. Understandably, Pinkie hesitated.

"Last I was here, ye dinna know if 'twas safe. Is it now? I care for ye friend, but I doona care for faeries. If I'm at risk, tell me now, and I will bid ye all goodbye."

He smiled and waved the man on through.

"'Tis fine, lad. I promise to keep ye safe."

———

*R*audrich apologized non-stop as we made the short ride up to the castle. It was unneeded. I'd seen the look of surprise on his face at the sound of his friend's voice. He had no idea they were coming.

Eventually, I couldn't bear to listen to him ramble on any further. I reached my hand up behind me to gently cup his face.

"It's okay. She clearly really needs to speak with you, or she wouldn't have come all this way. I'm rather tired anyway. I'll just slip away to your room when we get inside and leave you to them for the evening."

I felt the sharp intake of his breath against my back.

"Do ye…do ye wish me to stay in Calder's room, lass?"

"Definitely not. It's not like it will be our first time sleeping next to one another."

"Ach, thank God, lass. Knowing that I have yer warm arms to look forward to may be all that helps me survive the angry lassies that await me inside the castle. Doona wait up, though. I canna say how long they will keep me."

There was no way I would sleep, but I had no intention of letting him know just how much I would be anticipating his return to his bed.

"Okay, I won't. Hurry as fast as you can. It's a cold night. I need you to keep me warm."

He groaned and nibbled at my neck as he rode into the stables.

CHAPTER 34

*D*read settling in his gut at the angry expression on Sydney's face, Raudrich carefully closed the door to the sitting room and approached his friend.

"I know ye are angry with me, but at least give me a hug. I've missed ye, lass."

She stood with her arms crossed by the fire and stepped away as he reached for her.

"Don't touch me. Why did you ignore my letters? Why didn't you tell me about any of this? I've been worried about you for months, Raudrich. Do you know what I'm going to have to deal with when I get home? Callum is going to be furious with me. I knew he'd never let me leave to go looking for you if I told him. So I wrote to his brother and snuck off with him. I've made certain that Callum knew we were safe, but still…he won't be pleased. I've put my life on hold for you, and you're not even in danger, are you? You just…you just what? Decided to cut me out of your life? That's not how this works, Raudrich. You don't get to ghost me. We're not dating, you bloody imbecile."

Seeing that she needed to vent, Raudrich calmly took a seat by the fire and listened as she continued to scream at him.

"Is it that woman you were kissing? Is that it? You found yourself a girlfriend and decided you didn't need friends anymore? Is she the one who made you stop responding to my letters? How did I not know you were one of The Eight? Why didn't you tell me?"

The longer she screamed, the less angry she sounded. Slowly, her anger turned to tears. The moment she began to cry, Raudrich stood and moved to wrap his arms around her.

"Ach, Sydney, I'm sorry. I'm so, so sorry. I dinna mean to hurt or worry ye. 'Twas my pride that kept me from writing to ye. I dinna wish for ye to know the truth. I worried it would change how ye saw me, and there is none in the world that have such a high opinion of me as ye do."

She sniffled, and he tried not to grimace as she shamelessly wiped her nose on his shirt.

"What are you talking about?"

"Sit down and let me explain everything to ye."

With some coaxing, Sydney took her seat by the fire. Slowly, he told her everything—the reason he couldn't risk writing to her about The Eight and why he stopped writing to her because of his eyesight. When he finished, he couldn't help but ask her the one question on his mind.

"Why did ye come here, lass? Even if ye were worried, even if ye were mad, it still doesna explain why ye are here. Not when Silva must've told ye some of what she knew when ye arrived in Allen territory."

"You're right. I came here for Silva's sake. Obviously, I understand why you left in such a hurry now that you've explained everything, but you left her with a mess to clean up—one she never asked for. She doesn't want to be laird, Raudrich. She's still grieving the death of her husband. Allen territory wasn't even her home until a few years ago. She's miserable, and you gave her no choice before you left. You're going to fix this for her."

Such news surprised him. Silva was so strong, so capable. Despite the fact that his decision had been made in haste, he'd truly believed it the right one. Had he truly not even asked the lass if she was willing to be laird? If not, he owed her a great apology.

"I dinna know."

Sydney nodded and reached over to pat his hand.

"I know. So, that's what I'm going to tell Callum about why I came all this way, but the real reason is that I just really missed you, Raudrich. I wanted to see you. I wanted to see your home and make sure that you were okay. Are you okay? Are you happy?"

Happy was something he'd never placed much importance on, but for the first time in a very long time, happy did at least seem possible.

"I believe that I could be."

Sydney wiggled her eyebrows knowingly at him, and he laughed at how silly she looked.

"It's the girl, huh? She's very pretty. Although, she's quite shy, isn't she? I haven't heard her say a word."

He'd never seen anything in Laurel that made him believe she was shy.

"None of us gave her a chance to speak, did we? Ye'll like her. She's one of Morna's lassies, same as ye."

"Ah. I thought she looked, I don't know, out of time somehow. So...do you love her?"

"In truth, she's little more than a stranger to me still, but I do think that I could."

Sydney smiled and looked at him knowingly.

"If Morna sent her, you know you don't really have much of a choice right? Her matches always work out. I should know. Might as well not fight it or try to slow it down for manners' sake. If you feel it—which, from that slaphappy smile on your face, you do—just give in. You'll wind up in the same place either way. You may as well make the journey a little easier on yourself."

He suspected that Sydney was right, but he'd not say anything like that to Laurel just yet. The last thing he wanted to do was push her away by coming on too strongly.

"I doona doubt any of that, lass."

"Where's she at now?"

He could scarcely breathe each time he thought of it.

"In my bed."

Sydney's mouth fell open as she jumped up from the chair and moved to pull him to his feet.

"Then, what are you doing sitting around talking to me? We've got the daytime for that mess. Go and tend to your woman. Bed her well. Help her touch the heavens. Rock her world. Make her toes curl. You can totally do it."

Raudrich laughed at Sydney's bawdy remarks.

"Ach, lass, I'm sure that Pinkie dinna know what to do with ye. Ye do say the strangest things."

"It's what we out-of-time-lassies do, Raudrich. If I were you, I'd get used to it. I suspect you'll be hearing it for a very long time."

CHAPTER 35

J was still dressed and awake when Raudrich finally made it up to the room. He sighed at the sight of me sitting next to the dwindling fire when he entered.

"Ach, Laurel, ye truly dinna need to stay awake for my sake. I knew 'twas likely to take me some time to calm Sydney down. Ye must be bone-weary, lass. Stand and I'll tuck ye into bed nice and warm then I'll hold ye while ye sleep."

While I appreciated his thoughtfulness, I was still much too aroused from our journey back from the tavern to sleep. Standing, I walked over to him and reached to run my fingers through his hair.

"I do want you to hold me while I sleep, but if it's all well and fine by you, I'd like to do a few other things with you first."

I'd definitely had more ale than I'd realized. Either that or the characters I was trying my best to imitate had straight up decided to possess me. Such bluntness wasn't at all in my nature.

It felt nice, though. Perhaps, I should work on saying what I wanted more often.

And seeing the lift in his expression at my words made me

tingle with anticipation. He wanted me too, just as badly—possibly worse—than I wanted him.

"Are ye sure, lass? I'd consider it an honor to simply sleep next to ye. Ye needn't feel any obligation."

"Raudrich…" I stood on my tiptoes to reach him. After kissing him until he began to tremble, I trailed my lips toward his ear where I whispered, "I want you. I've already had you in my dreams, but tonight I want you in real life. I want to see you and taste you and feel you moving inside of me. Undress me and take me to your bed."

His response was immediate as he spun me away from him.

"This dress, lass, it suits ye."

I laughed as I looked down to see my breasts jiggling as he pulled at the laces of Freya's gown.

"It's too tight."

He bent to nip at my neck, his tongue warm against my neck.

"Precisely. Yer breasts barely stayed inside it while ye danced at the tavern. Every time I glanced at ye, all I wanted to do was taste them."

I gasped as his hand slipped inside the opening at the back of the gown and slid around my waist before slowly pushing upwards until he cupped both my breasts in his hands. He pushed outwards with his arms and in one quick sweep, the dress fell to the ground, leaving me naked and exposed to him.

I didn't move to cover myself. Instead, I leaned back into him as his hands roamed over me. He pulled me tight against him, and I could feel his erection pressing into my back as one hand dipped lower and deftly slipped into the warmth between my legs.

"Christ, lass, I have never wanted a woman so much."

I couldn't speak. My breath was coming too quickly. My heart was beating too fast for me to do anything but writhe against him.

He moved his fingers quickly until my knees buckled from

pleasure. As I began to tremble, he spun me toward him once again, quickly lifting me in his arms as I wrapped my legs around his waist and he carried me over to the bed.

The moment he lay me backwards, he removed his shirt and I reached for the tie on his breeches as I greedily slipped my hands inside to pull them downward.

I reached for him, taking his length in my hands as he groaned and bent to crush his mouth to mine.

The heat of his chest pressed against my bare skin only increased my need for him. Moving my hands to either side of his face, I kissed him as I spread my legs wide.

He felt me open myself to him and plunged inside as I screamed into his mouth.

We found our rhythm quickly. He took care to make sure that he matched his pace with my own, and when we both finally did climax, it was together.

It was hands down the best sex of my life, and from his endless exclamations I expected he would say the same come morning.

———

"*W*hy do ye write about love, lass?"

"Hmm…" I was half asleep when he spoke. We lay in just the same position I'd woken in several nights before. Tenderly, he twirled a lock of my hair with his fingers. "What was that?"

He lifted himself and my head dropped from his chest to the mattress as he propped himself up on his elbow.

"I asked why ye choose to write love stories."

"How do you even know that? I don't remember telling you that's what I wrote."

He smiled and immediately I knew.

"Ye dinna. Marcus told me."

Seeing in his expression that he really did wish to talk, I pushed myself up and moved to sit cross-legged on the bed as I pulled the blanket up with me for warmth.

"Almost everything is a love story at its core. The love story is just more central in the things that I write. It's what life is about, isn't it? We all have the same basic need to connect deeply with another person. I enjoy exploring that. I enjoy writing about all the different ways people can find love."

He was staring at me with great interest, and I could see that another question was right on the tip of his tongue.

"What?"

"Nothing, lass. Ye fascinate me, is all. If ye understand the value and importance of love so well, why then have ye resisted it so fiercely for most of yer life?"

"How do you…" I paused and shook my head. "Marcus again? Man, he was on a tear with you, wasn't he? What didn't he tell you about me?"

Raudrich laughed and leaned forward to kiss me quickly.

"He dinna tell me much, lass. And ye," he pointed at me playfully, "dinna answer the question."

I shrugged.

"I don't know, really. I guess I never found anyone that made the risk of getting hurt worth the possible reward."

He smiled at that.

"But I am?"

"It would seem so, wouldn't it? I've not been very successful at resisting you, at all."

With a flick of his wrist, he extinguished the flames in the fire and reached for me in the darkness. As we came together once more, he whispered into my ear.

"I'll not hurt ye, lass. Not now, nor ever if I can keep from it."

I didn't doubt the honesty in his words for a moment.

That didn't mean that I was safe in the least. But for once in my life, I simply didn't care.

Love with this man was worth it, no matter how risky.

CHAPTER 36

$\mathcal{I}$ woke only a few short hours after we fell asleep in each other's arms. While my body was deliciously exhausted, my mind was racing with a million different thoughts. There seemed to be an energy coursing through and around the castle, a foreboding feeling that left me uneasy and unable to rest. I wondered if Raudrich could feel it, as well. Although, from the look of him—arms spread wide across the bed, his mouth hanging open as he slept—he didn't look like it.

Carefully, I rolled away from his grip and rose from the bed as I quietly felt around on the floor for Freya's dress. I would've preferred to put on my own, but it was all the way across the castle in Marcus' room and I wasn't going to risk being spotted in the nude by our other guests.

Yanking the snug dress on, I tied the laces loosely and slipped quietly from the room.

I left the room with no real agenda—I just needed to move, to walk around in the hopes that some exercise might slow the jumble of thoughts inside my mind.

I'd yet to tell Kate what I knew I must. I was worried over Marcus and how he might or might not be adjusting to his new training and life. My thoughts were with Harry and the men who were searching for Calder. Even with my strong dislike for him, I hoped they would find him safe and well. I knew how strongly each of the men loved him.

There were other thoughts, too, happier ones—thoughts of Raudrich and the way I already knew what I felt for him but wouldn't allow myself to say out loud just yet.

His scent still clung to my skin, and the memory of our night spent together had me walking around the dark hallways of the castle with an embarrassingly goofy grin.

As I wandered, I reveled at how utterly quiet the castle was at night. All were asleep, all except Freya, of course.

I hesitated at the thought. I didn't know if Freya would welcome my company, but my curiosity eventually got the better of me as I paced back and forth in front of the castle's main door.

With Nicol away, Raudrich had said himself that Freya would be lonely. Perhaps, she would welcome the company.

I snuck into the nearest empty bedchamber—Paton's—to grab a blanket to wrap myself in while outside and realized right away why Raudrich had believed Paton would see reason to try and steal his room. The room—if one could even call it that—was little more than a closet. It had no real bed to speak of, only a simple sewn mattress and a small table next to the bed.

Laughing as I thought back on that night which now felt ages ago, I pulled the blanket from the bed and made my way outside.

The moon always seemed to be exceptionally bright on the isle and I was able to make my way to the garden path with ease. The crunch of dead leaves and plants crackled beneath my feet. So as not to frighten her, I called out to Freya and tried to hide the nervousness in my voice. I had no idea what to expect. I'd never seen a ghost before, let alone spoken to one.

"Freya, I'm Laurel. I don't know if Nicol mentioned me to you or not. I thought you might like some company. I was having a hard time sleeping."

I still couldn't see her, but she had the sweetest and most tender voice I'd ever heard.

"Aye, o'course, lass. Company doesna come to me easily. I never deny it when it does. Follow the path to yer left up ahead and ye will reach the garden's center. Ye shall see me right away when ye turn the corner."

I relaxed at her welcome and followed her directions with great anticipation. The moment I laid eyes on her, I couldn't help but gasp. Her translucent figure was breathtaking even from the height of Nicol's bedchamber window. In person, she was so beautiful it was almost difficult to look at her.

"Hi."

Freya smiled but didn't move from her seat as she waved me over to her.

"'Ello, lass. I hoped I would have the opportunity to visit with ye soon. Do ye know how long it has been since I've had the chance to visit with a woman?"

"Decades?"

She didn't look sad as she answered me and I was glad for it. It made it easier to be around her. It was heartbreaking anyway. If Freya appeared to be suffering or if she wallowed in despair, I wasn't sure I would've been able to stand it.

"Precisely, lass."

I moved to sit next to her and stared at her with wide eyes until she broke the silence.

"'Tis fine if ye wish to touch me, lass."

I was very curious.

"Will you feel it if I do?"

"No. Yer hand will sweep right through. Try. I promise ye, I doona mind."

Hesitantly, I reached as if I meant to shake her hand. It felt no different than waving it through air, though I could see my fingers pass through her own.

"Wow. I...I'm sorry, Freya. I can't begin to imagine what this is like for you."

She shrugged rather nonchalantly.

"I made my peace with this long ago, not that I willna welcome a release from this place when it comes. I pray for it every day."

"It will. Someday, you'll be free. I truly believe that."

She smiled and leaned in close.

"I agree, which is precisely why I am so verra glad that ye are here. It has restored my hope."

"Why do you say that? I've far less power than the men that surround you here. I can't see how I could possibly make you hope for anything."

She shook her head as she spoke up to disagree.

"Ye are wrong about that, Laurel. Yer presence here has agitated Machara in a way I've not ever felt before."

"That's only because," I hesitated. I hoped that saying Machara's suspicions out loud wouldn't give Freya any reason to believe them. "Machara worried that I might be here for Nicol. She's very jealous of him."

Freya laughed loudly.

"Lass, Marchara is a lying shrew. She no longer cares for Nicol. If she is ever free, she wouldna take him for herself. She would kill him without thought or feeling. This state she's placed me in, it ties me to her. I feel what she feels, and 'twas not jealousy she felt in yer presence. 'Twas fear."

"Why would she be afraid of me? I've no power over her."

"Why do ye think there are far more stories of faeries ruining the lives of men than of women?"

I hadn't the slightest idea.

"I don't know."

"Men would have us believe that we are the emotional ones, but they only tell themselves that to hide from what they know is true. We hold the power, lass. Faeries know this truth. They know that we are too wise to make the same bargains men strike with them all the time. The day Machara is defeated, it willna be at the hands of the men here. It shall be women that defeat her. Even now, with the two lassies that arrived this night, her fear has grown. With each new lass that steps inside the walls of this castle, Machara's chances of survival dwindle."

I liked the idea of that—Freya's certainty that it would be women that would save the day.

"How do you know that?"

"Because Machara does. She rarely permits herself to think on it, but I feel it each time fear flares up within her. It feels to me almost as if it were destined—a prophecy of sorts—one which she is determined to change. I doona believe she will."

"Have you ever mentioned any of this to Nicol?"

She shook her head, and for the first time all night, she looked sad.

"No. Nicol carries enough guilt for all that happened. His hope that one day he will free me is one of the few things that has made these years bearable for him. There's no need for him to know that it willna be him that saves me."

The sun was slowly beginning to peek over the horizon, and I could see in Freya's gaze that her night was almost over.

"Thank you for speaking with me. I'll visit you again."

She smiled and laid her hand on my knee, although I couldn't feel her touch.

"Oh, please do, Laurel. Even when Nicol returns, doona feel like ye canna interrupt him. I see enough of him. I would welcome yer company over his any time."

She disappeared while laughing. At least even in such a miserable purgatory, she'd found a way to be joyful.

She was a better woman than I ever hoped to be.

CHAPTER 37

*R*audrich was still asleep when I returned to the bedroom. I even went out of my way to wake him up, stomping around the room and flinging the curtains open so the sunrise would stream in. He didn't move. His soft snore just continued on.

Laughing, I moved over and crawled on top of the bed, crouching on both of my knees as I bent to kiss him.

"Hey you, wake up. I've been awake for hours now. You're going to sleep the whole day away."

He groaned and reached to pull me down toward him, snugly settling me into the space between his arm and chest.

"Laurel, why in God's name are ye already dressed? And what are ye talking about sleeping the day away? The sun is barely up. I must not have done a proper job of tupping ye last night. If I had, ye would wish to sleep until noon, at least."

I laughed as he nuzzled his lips on my ear, his breath tickling me until I started to writhe against him.

"Trust me, you did an excellent job. I'm just wound up. I'm not sure why."

He growled and turned to roll on top of me.

"Well then, lass, allow me to help ye unwind once more. Get out of that bloody dress. Ye look far better out of it. Why is it even on?"

He asked the question as he lifted my bum so that he could untie the laces and loosen them with his fingers. I didn't wish to think about how he must've gotten so deft at it. As my breasts sprang free from the top of the gown, he quickly pulled the dress to my feet.

"I..." I could barely talk as he bent and latched his teeth down on one of my nipples. "I went to speak to Freya."

He quickly glanced up at me before moving his lips downward, kissing the side of my waist between words.

"Freya...why...did...ye...wish...to...speak...with...her?"

I was squirming now. My hips rising of their own volition as my body began to ache for him. I wanted him inside me, wanted to move with him as we'd done only hours before.

"Holy crap, Raudrich. I can't think when your tongue is..." I cried out as he kissed me between my legs. Reaching for his hair, I pulled him up to me and quickly rolled him over so I could straddle him. I needed him. Now.

"Can we talk about Freya later?"

"Fine by me, lass."

I came down on him hard and heavy, and the cry that escaped his lips as I began to move on top of him quickly escalated my own climax. There was nothing slow in our exploration of each other this time. It was rough and needy, and when we finally came apart, I was trembling with exhaustion.

"Do ye wish to sleep now, lass? Please say aye, for I doona think I have the strength to tup ye again just now."

I laughed as my eyelids grew heavy.

"I actually feel like I could sleep. Well done."

He laughed as I turned onto my side and snuggled my bare bum and feet against him.

Just as my eyes began to close, Sydney's annoyingly chipper voice called to us through the door.

"Wake up you two. I'm sure you're tired from all the boom-boom I hope you guys did last night, but I made breakfast, and it's getting cold fast."

Sydney's meal was by far the best I'd had since arriving in this time, and I found myself feeling quite jealous of the residents of Cagair Castle who had their very own professional chef to cook their meals.

I sat next to her throughout breakfast. While Raudrich visited with Griffith and Silva, we had a chance to talk about some things only those acquainted with Morna could truly relate to.

"So, how'd she send you back? Did she at least ask your permission first?"

I asked the question as I shoveled yet another bite of frittata into my mouth.

"Oh, that's quite a long story. She actually didn't want me to know about the magic. She wasn't sure I could be trusted. So she spelled my coffee with some sort of truth serum and then once she was convinced I wasn't under the command of some evil witch she had history with, she allowed Callum, my husband, to take me through the stairwell."

"Stairwell?" That sounded much more pleasant than being tossed into a pile of hay in a smelly stable.

"Yes. Cagair's time-travel contraption wasn't actually created by Morna, and it's much easier on the body than the way she always goes about it. You can just walk back and forth between this century and our own."

"What?"

I couldn't hide the astonishment and excitement in my voice. It was like hearing that I'd won the lottery and would stay young for the rest of my life at the same time. If Sydney was telling me the truth, it meant I could see Kate again. Whether I wished to go forward, or she back, I didn't have to say goodbye to my sister forever. It also gave Marcus more options for the rest of his life, once the curse was broken.

Sydney's expression as she looked at me was one of concern.

"Did you think you were trapped here, Laurel? Is that what Morna told you?"

In truth, I guess Morna hadn't said those exact words, but her glib farewell through her letter had sure made it seem that way.

"Yes, I did think that. She didn't say that outright, but she did tell me that she was finished communicating with me. I didn't think there was a way to return home without her."

Sydney shook her head and I got the feeling that even if things tended to turn out well for the women Morna sent back, each of them had their own feelings of frustration toward the meddling witch who had so intrusively upended their lives.

"Morna means well. She truly, always does, but sometimes, I don't agree with the way she goes about things. I'm much fonder of her husband, Jerry. I don't care what Morna made you think. The rest of us go forward and back all of the time, and I'll be damned if you don't have the same option that we do. Listen," she paused and reached to grab my hand. I felt like I might cry at the relief that was slowly flooding my entire system. "If you need to go forward or if someone you love needs to come back, just come to Cagair. It's quite a long journey, but you are welcome any time. I'll walk you through myself. That passageway isn't Morna's. She has no claim on it and no say on how it is used."

I threw my arms around her with no regard for how odd we must look to the rest of the table.

"Are you sure? It...it doesn't put you guys in danger in any way?"

She pulled back just far enough to look at me.

"We keep it well hidden, but any girl that gets pulled into Morna's shenanigans needs some say in her own life. The stairwell is yours—Cagair is yours—any time you need it."

"Thank you." I pulled her in for another short hug before quickly pushing myself away from the table to stand. "Thank you so much. I'm sorry to be rude, but there's something I have to take care of right away."

I couldn't sit at the table a moment longer. I had a phone call to make—one that I no longer dreaded.

CHAPTER 38

*K*ate picked up on the second ring. I'd never been so thrilled to hear her voice.

"Hello?"

"Kate, it's me. Step into a room that Mom isn't in, okay?"

I could hear the quick shuffle of her feet followed by the sound of a door closing before she squealed into the phone.

"Oh, my God, Laurel! You're okay? You're safe? Are you really...are you really in the past? How the hell are you calling me?"

Smiling, I slid down to the floor on the other side of Raudrich's bedroom door and leaned against it as I answered her.

"Yes, yes, and yes, to your first three questions. I'm okay. I'm safe. And I'm speaking to you from the year sixteen hundred and fifty-one. As for how I'm calling you...you can thank the same magical witch that sent me to this time for that."

"Oh, I will. Laurel, I have so much to tell you. You know as well as I do that I've got way too much time on my hands." She paused and snickered. "Or, I guess I should really say hand. Anyway, way too much time with nothing to do. From the second

213

you and Marcus left for the airport, all I could think about was where you were going and what you would be seeing, so I decided to do some research. Where are you exactly? Are you at Conall Castle or are you on the Isle of Eight Lairds?"

I smiled into the phone. She sounded more like her old self. It was really good that she was able to make a joke about her injury without crying.

"Wow, Kate. You must either be really bored, or Mom must be driving you up the wall for you to have done research. Which is it?"

I was the book worm. Kate definitely was not. Kate had read my first novel out of obligation only. Besides that, I wasn't sure she'd picked up a book since college. Not that I would ever complain about her doing research on this time. It was bound to come in handy. Perhaps Kate would be able to provide me with some of the answers Morna had been so unwilling to give.

"Honestly, it's neither. It was just that when you left, I couldn't shake the feeling—even as crazy as it seemed at the time—that this whole thing was actually real. If it was, I knew this had to be something pretty momentous, ya know? So I just started looking up what I could find about both places. So, tell me, where are you?"

"The Isle of Eight Lairds."

Her voice was giddy with excitement. "Oh, good! I learned way more about that place anyway. Laurel, I haven't slept in days. It's going to take me weeks to come down from the amount of caffeine and chocolate I've consumed since you left. I've been working my way through everything I could find on that place like a maniac. Are you sitting down? I have some seriously serious shit to tell you."

"I am." I'd called believing that I would be the one doing most of the talking. I was quickly getting the feeling that I was wrong.

"Okay, good. Let me think about where I should begin. I wasn't really expecting to hear from you, so I'm not prepared. I was actually just planning on telling you in person."

I quickly interrupted her. "In person?"

"Yeah, in person. Do you really think for a second that after all I've learned that I was going to leave you there alone? No way, girlfriend. I already have flights booked for me, Mr. Crinkles, Mom, and Marcus' dad to Edinburgh in three weeks. I would've booked them sooner but David couldn't get off work before then."

My brain couldn't possibly keep up with the totally unexpected news she was dumping on me. "Hang on. You need to slow down. Mom and David know where Marcus and I are? What did you tell them to make them believe you? I can't imagine either of them took that news well. And more than that, how were you going to get back here when you got to Edinburgh?"

Kate took a deep breath. I suspected that she realized she'd started to let herself run away with things in her excitement. When she spoke again, her tone was calm and collected.

"I'm not an idiot, Laurel. I did tell Mom and David where I thought you were, but I obviously didn't tell either one of them that you were chilling hundreds of years in the past. And I figured we'd get back the same way you did. We'd go looking for Morna."

"How did you get them to agree to go with you?"

"That was trickier, but I told them that you guys had decided to stay in Scotland for the rest of the summer and you wanted everyone together to celebrate Marcus' birthday at the end of the month. When I told them that I would foot the bill, they happily agreed."

I nodded, my thoughts suddenly drifting to what a pain in the butt my mother would be while adjusting to this time. I dreaded the thought of her being here, but I also knew that if Kate was planning to join me here, we could hardly just disappear off the face of the earth without telling her. We were her world, and despite her helicopter nature, we both loved her dearly.

"How can you afford that?"

Kate laughed into the phone. "I can't, but what does it matter? I'll not be coming back here, and I doubt they're going to be able to find me to haul me off to debtor's prison in the seventeenth century."

"Kate." Now, I was worried. I wanted to see Kate, but this was too big of a decision for her to make on a whim. "You can't possibly know that you'll want to be here forever. You don't need to do anything that will ruin your life back home."

"Oh, I do know that I'll be there forever. You will, too."

"How can you possibly know that?"

"Laurel, you really should've read that book you found. Marcus wasn't the only one inside it. I'm pretty sure you were, too. And unless there's another one-handed, burn-victim with a black cat there at the castle with you now, I'm in the book, too."

CHAPTER 39

*J*t took me a good thirty seconds to respond to her. You would think after so many unbelievable things occurring over the past week, I would've been past the point of being surprised. I wasn't.

"Okay, Kate. You're going to need to explain everything you've read from the beginning. I'm just going to sit back and listen. I'm feeling slightly light-headed."

My sister laughed and as I settled into my spot on the floor, I could hear Mr. Crinkles purr in the background.

"Okay, I can't blame you for that. It's a lot, and some of it's not so great."

"I'm ready." I was anything but.

"So, I read the book first, start to end. You know how history gets twisted throughout time and then you throw in a few ancient legends and things get even worse, so I have no idea how much of what I read is true, but I'll try to explain the gist of it to you."

I nodded as if she could see me. "Okay, shoot."

"The documentary told us about the legend, right—about The Eight and how they were bound to protect the Isle from the darkness that would threaten it if The Eight were ever broken? The book was much more specific. According to this text, the evil the documentary mentioned is a faerie. While she may gain strength, she poses no real threat with just seven men."

I interrupted to give her some context.

"The book is right. It is a faerie."

"All right, then. That makes me even more confident about everything else. Anyway, as I was saying, if The Eight become seven, that's not necessarily good, but nothing too bad will happen. Six is the magic number. Six is what she's aiming for. If The Eight lose two men without replacing another, she can break free from her prison."

I thought of Calder's disappearance. It was a good thing Marcus' powers had revealed themselves when they did. It was possible that Calder could find a way to break his bind to the men at any time. If he'd managed to do that before Marcus had joined them, Machara would've been free.

Kate paused for a moment, and I assumed she was waiting for me to react.

"That coincides with some things that have already happened here. Continue."

"Okay. What's the name of this faerie? Do you know?"

"Yes, I do. I met her. Her name is Machara."

I could hear Kate's smile in her voice.

"This is all just too flipping cool. The book got that right, too. So, the book alludes to a prophecy given to Machara by her father as punishment for something she'd done to anger him. It doesn't say what. He claimed that a time would come in Machara's life when she would be chained by the magic of men, but her life would end at the hands of mortal women."

Freya's prediction came to my mind. "How many women and when?"

Kate sighed. "Nine women, and there is no date listed in the story."

Of course it didn't.

"Okay, does it say anything about these women. Who are they?"

"That's where you come in, Laurel. You're one of them, and I'm pretty sure, so am I."

The hairs on my arms rose, and I was suddenly very cold.

"Explain."

"Your name isn't mentioned specifically. It only refers to a Laird Allen's wife, which is beyond annoying, I know. Women shouldn't be defined by their husbands, but I'm pretty sure this book was written in the sixties, so we'll just have to forgive it and move on."

My heart beat quickly in my chest.

"I'm not Laird Allen's wife."

"Maybe not yet, but if the rest of this book is to be believed, you're going to be. The woman's description matches you exactly."

It was a real struggle to keep from giggling like an idiot. It was too soon for me to dream of such things with Raudrich, but there was some part of me that knew it was inevitable.

"Okay." I tried to keep my tone calm. "For theory's sake, let's say that it is me. What does it say?"

"That you're the first of the nine women who will ultimately destroy Machara, but that each woman will be tested in her own time and in her own way."

Awesome. I'd never been a very good test taker.

"Does it say how I will be tested?"

"This doesn't, but I found something else that I think does."

"Okay, let's finish with the book first. What does it say of the other women? How do you know that you're one of them?"

"It wasn't even in the main text of the book. It doesn't go into detail about the nine women, but there was an author footnote at the bottom of one of the pages. I don't remember the exact wording, but it said something along the lines of: *little is known of the women who lifted the castle's curse, though two of the nine were believed to be sisters, both blonde of hair and blue of eyes, though one had suffered much at the hands of a fire."*

I sat silently for a few seconds.

"That's an oddly specific footnote."

"I know, right?"

And then, at the exact same time, we both said,

"Morna."

Laughing, I continued.

"Exactly. How much do you want to bet that she added that little piece of information just for you?"

"I'd say the chances are pretty good."

"Is that all you learned from the book?"

There was a brief pause as Kate took a deep breath.

"Pretty much, but the article is what you really need to strap in for, sis. I think it involves you. It was an article about the fall of one of The Eight—the only one who is ever believed to have died of something other than natural causes."

A lump rose in my throat. I didn't even want to ask the question, but I knew that I had to. Silently, praying that she wouldn't say Raudrich's name, I spoke. "Does it have the man's name?"

"A Laird Bracht."

I only knew each of them by their first names. At least I knew it wasn't Raudrich.

"Does it describe him?"

"It does. It describes him as being a tall and slender man in his late-twenties at the time of his death. He supposedly had raven black hair and piercing blue eyes."

The air left my chest in a whoosh.

"It's Calder. What does it say?"

He was in his late-twenties now. If the article was true, Calder didn't have much time left.

"Supposedly, this man of The Eight—Calder, I suppose—was seduced by a faerie he met on the shores of the isle. After sleeping with her, his lust for her became unquenchable, and he thought himself in love. In his desperation to be with her, he went to the faerie with whom his magic was bound—Machara—and begged her to turn him into one of the fae. As faeries so often do, she offered him a deal. In his blind need, he took it without thought."

I shivered and held the phone up to my ear with my shoulder as I wrapped my arms around my knees for warmth.

"What was the deal?"

"She made him promise that he would surrender the first woman to grace the steps of the castle into her care. In exchange, she would make it so that he could be with the woman he loved."

I was the first woman permitted inside the castle in years, but Calder had made no move to bring me to Machara.

"What else does it say?"

"Well, here's the thing you need to know about faeries, Laurel. I've discovered this during my days of researching them. They keep their word, but only to the degree that they must. If there is a way for them to twist it, to turn what you want against you, they will find it. This is what Machara did with this man. She didn't promise him that she would turn him into a faerie. She promised that she would make it so that they could be together.

"The article says that rather than turn Calder fae, she turned the faerie into a human. There is no worse punishment for one of the fae. In her despair, the woman Calder loved threw herself off the isle's tallest cliff, plunging to her death."

Calder's angry disposition suddenly made so much more sense. So did his belief that I was horribly unattractive. I supposed for a man in love with a faerie, I wasn't quite up to par.

"Oh, my gosh, Kate. That's horrible."

"That's not all. In his rage, he confronted Machara and swore to her that he wouldn't keep his word, but she simply laughed. He'd given his oath to her in blood. She told him that she had the power to control him at will, that when a woman did arrive at the castle, he wouldn't be able to ignore the call to bring the woman to Machara."

"That's why he ran." I whispered the words under my breath, as the pieces of the puzzle clicked into place.

"What?"

"Calder ran away from the castle days ago. The men thought he wished to break his bind to them, but he was just trying to protect me. He was trying to escape Machara's power over him before she forced him to bring me to her."

Kate's voice was sad and filled with worry as she spoke.

"Well, for your sake, I hope he stays gone. If he returns, I'm not sure there's much you'll be able to do to stop him from giving you to Machara."

I hoped so, too, but I'd never been very lucky. I didn't expect that would change anytime soon.

CHAPTER 40

"*I* promise ye, Silva. I will think of a solution soon, and when I do, I shall return home to see ye relieved of yer duties as laird. Ye will then be free to leave. I dinna know 'twas so painful for ye to be there."

I stood far back from Raudrich and Silva, but I could still hear his promise to her as he prepared to bid her farewell. The entire group of travelers was leaving today, then Raudrich and I truly would have the castle to ourselves for the next few weeks.

After seeing Silva settled on her horse, Raudrich moved to bid Pinkie and Griffith goodbye. As I stood there watching them, Sydney gently tapped me on the shoulder.

"Hey, come over here a second. I want to talk to you before we leave."

I needed to speak with her, as well. Together, we walked to the edge of Freya's garden, out of earshot and sight of Raudrich.

"I was wanting to speak to you too, actually. It seems that I may be taking you up on your offer of hospitality sooner rather than later, if that's still okay? My sister means to travel back with our Mom and the father of my dearest friend. You haven't met him."

Sydney's face lit up at the news.

"Of course, it's okay. It will give me another excuse to visit you all here. Next time, I'll bring Callum. I will see your sister and family through then Callum and I will escort them here. I'll work on helping them make the adjustment, too. It's never easy—realizing that all of this could be true."

"Thank you so much, Sydney. I'm so happy to have met you. Now, what did you want to talk to me about?"

She fidgeted nervously from foot to foot for a moment before finally straightening herself as if she'd finally worked up the nerve to say what she wished.

"Well, Laurel, I'm not really looking forward to saying anything about this to you, but Raudrich's worth it, so for just a moment I'm going put aside my scruples and pretend I'm Morna for a minute and meddle. Raudrich is one of the most loyal men I've ever known. If he's important to you, there is absolutely nothing he wouldn't do for you. He's all in with you, Laurel, I can tell. But I don't quite get the same read from you. You're happy, sure, but you don't look like a woman who is crazy in love.

"If I've learned anything from my time in this century and with these people, it's this: everything can change in a second. So, if you feel the same for him as he does for you, don't wait to tell him. Don't hold yourself back just because you're scared. As you and I both know, time is a pretty relative concept anyway. Who cares if this happened quickly? That doesn't make it any less right."

I knew Sydney was right. Even as Kate had laid my destiny out before me, I resisted it. I was scared. I was scared that in the end he might change his mind. I was scared that somehow I wouldn't be enough.

It was time for me to get over my fears. It was time for me to grow up.

*L*aurel was restless. From the moment Sydney and the others had left until they sat down for an evening meal, he'd watched as she paced around the castle, straightening things that didn't need to be straightened and dusting things that were entirely free of dust.

She was nervous about something, and he didn't know whether to pry or allow her whatever space she might need.

Eventually, as her fingers drummed over and over against the table while they ate, Raudrich couldn't contain his concern any longer.

"Laurel, lass, ye've not stopped moving once all day. If there is something wrong, I wish ye would tell me."

"Nothing's the matter."

She continued to drum her fingers over and over.

"I doona believe ye. Yer mind is elsewhere. Was it Freya? We never did get an opportunity to speak of what she said to ye. I've always known her to be a kind and friendly sort of woman, but mayhap she was different with ye?"

Laurel's fingers stopped their assault on the table as she looked up at him in surprise.

"Not at all. Freya was great."

It would've surprised him if Laurel had said otherwise, but it was the only thing he could think of. Unless… "'Twas Sydney, aye? Ach, what did she say to ye? I am sorry if she was unkind. She is like a sister to me—she can be verra protective."

Laurel's expression remained confused. "Sydney's great, too."

An unusual emotion was starting to build within him. It had been so long since he'd felt it, he almost didn't recognize it —insecurity.

"If 'twas not Freya and 'twas not Sydney, then it must be me, lass. What did I do to upset ye? Do ye not wish to be here? Have ye tired of me already?"

For the first time in hours, Laurel really looked at him. As she smiled, his worries slowly faded away.

She stood from the table with a mischievous gleam in her eye and walked over toward him. He pushed his chair away from the table and stood to greet her as she stepped into his embrace and wrapped her arms around his waist.

"I'm not upset. There's nowhere else in the world I want to be. And with every minute I spend with you, I become more and more sure of the fact that I'll never grow tired of being around you." Laurel paused and lifted her head so that her chin rested against his chest as she looked up at him. He loved the way her blue eyes sparked in the candlelight. "And do you know what else?" She didn't wait for him to respond. "You're kind of cute when you're worried."

"I wasna worried, lass. 'Tis only that I wouldna wish to keep ye here if ye dinna want to stay."

He tried to argue, but he knew his expression had given everything away.

"I do want to stay. And you can deny it all you want, but you were worried just now. I don't want you to worry ever again, Raudrich."

His heart began to hammer painfully in his chest. There were only three words he wished to hear from her, but he didn't know if she had it in her to trust him so completely just yet.

"Aye?"

"You don't have to say anything back. I want you to know that. I know this has all happened very quickly, and if someone had told me a week ago I'd be about to say this to you now, I would've called them crazy..."

He couldn't bear it another moment. Pulling away, he placed

one finger across her lips to silence her before reaching to cup her face as he placed his forehead against hers.

"I'm in love with ye, lass. I doona care if I doona know yer last name or yer favorite season. I'll gladly spend the rest of my life learning all that I can about ye. I'm a man who has always known my own heart, lass, and I knew right away that mine belonged to ye. Marry me. Marry me and make this castle yer home for good."

She answered him with a kiss and a squeal. And right there in the empty dining hall, he got the dance he'd been denied the night before.

He'd not known such happiness could exist.

Why then did he feel such dread?

wo Weeks Later

audrich and I spent the two weeks following his proposal enjoying every minute of our time alone. We visited, laughed, ate, and made love. We went on regular horseback rides around the isle where Raudrich took his time telling me the history of the isle and its people. I told him all about Morna's phone and Kate's plan to join us here, and we agreed that we should wait until she was here to begin plans for our wedding.

Each evening, I would spend a few hours with Freya. Selfishly, the more time I spent with her, the more I realized how sad I would be when the day finally did come that she was free of Machara's curse.

On the fifteenth day after the men left, Freya made mention of Machara's shift in mood. While Freya could see no reason for it, I had my own suspicions. There was only one thing that I could see that would lift Machara's mood—the men had succeeded in finding Calder and he was already back on the isle.

My suspicion was proven correct the following morning when Harry, Maddock, and Nicol returned to the castle with Calder. They had him bound and gagged. He looked terrible, nothing like himself as he thrashed about and tried to fight his way free.

Harry looked devastated by Calder's state. None of the men could make sense of his behavior.

I understood it perfectly. He wasn't evil underneath, and he was fighting the evil that controlled him with everything he had.

The weeks of relative quiet around the castle left me with plenty of time to think through Calder's story and all the unanswered questions it posed. Why did Machara want me? And if Calder fulfilled his promise to Machara by delivering me to her, what would be the cause of his death?

It was thinking back on that night down in the dungeon that made the answer clear to me. Machara truly had wished to see the depth of my affection for Raudrich and his for me. She'd been too pleased at the obvious attraction between us for her reaction to have been an act. I could see only one reason why she would even care—if Raudrich loved me, he would do anything for me—even sacrifice his own life to save me.

But seven members wouldn't be enough to free Machara from her cell, and that explained why Calder would have to die, too. The men were already bound to Machara through their magic, but Calder's bargain with her allowed her to control him. Killing him would be as easy as giving him the directive to do the job himself.

If she could make Raudrich sacrifice himself to save me, and if she could order Calder to kill himself before their bargain was complete, then The Eight would be six and Machara would be free.

I would never let that happen. I could see no way of saving Calder, but I sure as hell was going to save Raudrich.

I had a plan—a risky one—one that would require the help of every member of The Eight, save two.

"*L*aurel?"

I dropped the quill at the sound of Marcus' voice in the doorway. I was busy writing a letter—one that I hoped Raudrich would never have to see.

Slowly, I turned to him, unsure of what to expect. There was every reason in the world for him to still be angry with me.

He looked good—really good. His stature was tall, his shoulders broad, and his expression seemed relaxed and even, dare I say, happy?

"Marcus." I stood and all but ran to him, but pulled up short before throwing myself into his arms until I saw him open them to me.

When he did, I nearly knocked him down with my enthusiasm.

"Are you still angry? I really am sorry, Marcus."

My cheek was pressed flush against his chest, but I felt him shrug as I held him.

"Yes, a little, but it's okay."

I pulled away just enough to look up at him. "Really?"

He smiled and I relaxed into him once more.

"Really. It's very odd, Laurel. Logically, I know that I shouldn't be okay with this, but the magic has messed with my head. It's shifted who I am. This is right, somehow. This is where I'm supposed to be."

I nodded against him. "Me, too. I have something to tell you."

I pulled him inside the bedroom and closed the door so we could talk. For the rest of the day, we exchanged stories. I told him of my engagement and of Kate and, most importantly, of how his father would be on his way here by the end of the month. He cried at that, and my heart could've just burst right then and there from the joy I felt at seeing his relief that he wouldn't be forever separated from his favorite person in all the world. Marcus' dad outshone even me in Marcus' eyes.

Then he told me all that he'd learned and even showed off his new skills with a few acts of magic he couldn't have been more proud of.

It was a lovely afternoon, but it was all I could do to keep from wondering...

What if this was the last afternoon I would ever spend with him? I couldn't bear to think of it, but I knew there was a good chance it could be true.

I had to go through with my plan tonight. And there was every possibility in the world things wouldn't end well for me.

CHAPTER 42

"*M*addock?"

I found him in the stables tending to the horse I'd developed a fondness for during my first night here.

"Laurel!" He turned toward me at the sound of my voice and quickly dropped the brush he held in his hands to run toward me with open arms, quickly scooping me up into a bear hug of an embrace as he spun me around in a circle. "Congratulations on yer happy news. I canna tell ye how pleased I am that ye will be here with us forever."

For a moment, I was able to forget about what I knew was coming, and I smiled as he returned me to my feet.

"Thank you, Maddock. Listen, I need your help with something. It's urgent."

"Anything, lass. Ye are one of us now. There is not a one of us who wouldna do anything for ye."

"That's what I'm counting on. I need to meet with all of you, but Raudrich and Marcus absolutely cannot be there. Is there a way we can arrange that?"

He looked at me for a long moment, and I suspected he could see the fear in my eyes.

"Aye. I'll have Harry place them both on Calder watch. We canna leave him alone. 'Tis the strangest thing I've ever seen. He is mad with his desire to leave here."

I nodded. "I know. We need to meet as soon as possible."

"After dinner, I'll ask them both to keep watch. We will meet ye in the dining hall then."

*T*hey didn't like it, but I could see by their resigned expressions that there were no other options.

Maddock was the least receptive, which didn't surprise me. He and I shared a bond of sorts, one that I'd noticed from the first day we met.

"Lass, I doona care for this. Faeries are too unpredictable. If anything happened to ye, Raudrich would never forgive us. We would never forgive ourselves for agreeing to help ye with this."

"If any of you have another suggestion, I'm open to it."

"I do, lass." Harry spoke up from the end of the table, and I wanted to cry just by looking at him. He looked ill, heartbroken, and weary. "We keep Calder bound. We imprison him until she loses her patience and kills him. We can keep him from ye."

I'd already considered that possibility.

"I'm sorry, but no. The moment Calder hands me over to her, she will kill him. If we prevent him from following her order, she's likely to do something worse. I couldn't live with it if Calder wound up like Freya because of me."

"I'll do as ye bid, lass. I'll make certain that neither Raudrich or Marcus interfere. What say the rest of ye?"

I appreciated Ludo's interjection. There was no sense in debating.

"Thank you, Ludo."

Slowly, one by one, they all agreed, and our plan was set.

Maddock would relieve Raudrich and Marcus of their watch duty over Calder. I would go to bed like always and slip out as Raudrich slept. We all knew Raudrich would follow as soon as he realized I was gone. The others would be ready to follow him.

J lingered longer than I planned, but leaving Raudrich's bed was the most difficult thing I'd ever had to do. I felt as if my life were just beginning. I sincerely hoped that it wouldn't be over so soon.

Picking up the letter I'd written earlier to give to Maddock, I lifted the quill one last time and wrote Raudrich a note that I left upon his pillow.

Don't blame the men. None of them wanted to do this. It will be okay. If it's not, just know that you showed me what I never knew men could be. You've given me the best few weeks of my life. I love you. – Laurel

With one soft kiss while he slept, I left him.

CHAPTER 43

*H*arry, not Maddock, sat outside the room where they held Calder. His eyes were red. He'd been crying.

"It must be me who sets him free, lass. I need to be the last one he sees. I need him to know that we forgive him, that we love him."

Without a word, I took a seat on the floor next to him and wrapped my arm around his shoulders. He gave me one painful glance and then allowed himself to cry on my shoulder.

We sat like that for a long time. When Harry finally lifted his head from my shoulder, he leaned forward and kissed my cheek.

"I doona care for grief, lass. Promise me that ye will do all that ye can to return to us. Doona make me go through this heartbreak twice."

I swallowed the lump in my throat and tried to keep my voice steady. "I'll find a way out. Don't you worry about that."

Clearing his throat, Harry stood and offered me his hand and pulled me to my feet.

"Laurel, I doona know just how tied Calder is to Machara. I think it best ye doona allow him to know of yer plan in case she can hear his thoughts. Fight him when he comes for ye."

"I will."

He stepped inside the room without another word. I moved to the main stairwell to wait.

"*I*'m sorry, lass. I'm so, so sorry. I doona wish to do this. 'Tis why I tried to get ye to leave. Ye must know that I doona have a choice."

Calder's grip on my arms was rough as I thrashed about. He was as strong as an ox. The more I tugged and pulled, the more I screamed and bit, the rougher his grip on my arms became as he dragged me. I would have bruises all over, but I was committed to my performance.

"Let me go, Calder. Please. I'll leave. I promise. Just let me go."

We were in Nicol's bedchamber now, and I could hear Machara's laughter echoing up from the dungeon.

"'Tis too late for that, lass."

He opened the passageway and down we went. He continued to beg my forgiveness.

"If I could stop this, I would."

I needed Calder to know that I understood. I wanted him to have a little bit of peace before his death. I only hoped that I would be able to tell him quickly enough before Machara took me so she wouldn't hear and understand.

I squeezed his arm and pulled to get his attention. He quickly turned tortured eyes on me.

"It's okay. I know." I mouthed the words to him, and just as we stepped into Machara's view, I could see that he understood. He now knew why Harry had released him.

He nodded and released his grip, throwing me before Machara's cell as he spoke to her.

"Here. Now, let me go, Machara. I've done as ye bid. Take her and release me."

I looked into Machara's icy eyes and shivered. There was no humanity in her gaze.

She quickly jerked her head upward, and I saw the panic settle over Calder's face. I knew that his death was imminent.

Just as Machara uttered the spell that would pull me into the cell with her, Calder—his hands trembling as he tried to resist—lifted his sword and plunged it into his heart.

CHAPTER 44

"*W*here did ye go, lass? Ye've moved too far away from me and my side has grown cold. Come closer."

Half-asleep, Raudrich reached for Laurel, only to find the space next to him empty.

Concerned, he sat up to look around the room, but Laurel was nowhere inside. The blankets on her side of the bed were still warm. She couldn't have been gone long, but where would she have gone?

The rest of the men were asleep, and with Nicol now back, she'd not have reason to keep Freya company. He didn't often worry, but the air felt unusually heavy this night, as if it held a warning of something he couldn't yet see.

Doing his best to remain calm, Raudrich rose and lit a fire as he began to dress. It was only once the room was illuminated by the glow of fire that he noticed the small piece of parchment on Laurel's pillow.

He read her words with trembling hands as he rattled his mind and tried to make sense of what she could mean.

Panic coursing through him, he ran out into the hallway. Harry stood only a few steps away from his door.

"What is this? Where is she?"

He thrust the note in Harry's face as his lifelong friend began to cry.

"I'm sorry, Raudrich. We had no choice, truly."

He grabbed Harry by the collar of his shirt, yanking him roughly toward him.

"What do ye mean ye dinna have a choice? Tell me what has happened, Harry."

A sudden pain shot through his chest, so sharp and staggering he fell to his knees in agony. Harry did the same, and for a few brief seconds, all either man could do was scream.

The pain disappeared as quickly as it had come. The change in the magic around them was palpable—one of The Eight was dead.

As Harry began to sob, Raudrich knew—Calder.

"Where is he? Where is Laurel?"

"The dungeon, lad. There is nothing ye can do. We canna allow ye to save her."

He pushed himself to his feet and ran toward Nicol's bedchamber as Machara's blood-curdling laughter reverberated up from the floor.

"Let her be safe, let her be safe."

The prayer played itself over and over in his mind as he ran. As he pushed open the door to the dungeon, he had to lean against the wall to keep himself steady.

The space below reeked of death and blood, and he could hear nothing save Machara's laughter.

Bracing, he turned the corner to find Calder's lifeless body only a short distance in front of him. He was on his knees, held up by his sword, which ran through him. Calder's head hung painfully forward as blood drained from his chest.

Swallowing the bile rising in his throat, Raudrich raised his gaze from the floor to stare into Machara's cell. She stood in the center of the small space, and Laurel was on her knees in front of her. Machara's hands were around Laurel's throat.

"There ye are, lad. I knew it wouldna take ye long."

He said nothing. He was too busy looking Laurel up and down for a sign of injury. There was no blood or open wound. Despite Machara's grip around her neck, she appeared unharmed. He would have to proceed carefully to ensure that she remained that way.

"Laurel, lass. I'll not…"

Machara squeezed her fingers around Laurel's neck and he stopped short of what he meant to say. As he stopped speaking, she relaxed her grip.

"Doona speak with her, lad. If ye say another word to her, or she to ye, I'll slip this nail deep into her vein, and I'll let her bleed out in front of ye. This mortal is simply a pawn. The bargain must be struck between ye and I."

"What do ye want, Machara?"

"What I've always wanted. My freedom. With Calder dead, only one more death is required to free me. Ye love her. I can see that. But do ye love her more than ye love yerself? More than ye love the men ye are bound to through yer oath?"

Without another thought, he walked over to Calder's body and pulled the sword from his friend's lifeless chest.

Returning to stand directly in front of Machara, he turned the blade toward his own chest.

"This is what ye want, aye? My own death, as well as Calder's? If I do this, do ye swear to me, ye shall let Laurel go?"

"Aye, lad, I swear to ye. If ye run yerself through with that sword, I will leave the lass unharmed."

Just as he pressed the tip of the blade into his chest, the world went dark around him. He fought against the spell. He could hear the chants of the other men in his mind, but their combined magic was too strong for him to fight against it.

The sword flew out of his hands as he collapsed into unconsciousness.

If Laurel was dead when he woke, he would kill every last one of his men.

---

*M*achara screamed as Raudrich fell. For a moment, I worried she would snap my neck without another thought.

Instead, she whirled on me, quickly pulling me up by my wrists as she threw me against the wall.

"What did ye do?"

I'd not known how The Eight would stop Raudrich, but the moment I saw him fall, I knew what I needed to do. It would require that I put on a play for Machara once again.

I was more terrified than I'd ever been in my life, but I couldn't allow Machara to see that. She wouldn't believe the callous performance I meant to give her if she saw my fear.

Freya was right. The hubris of faeries was their downfall. They didn't believe they could lose, so they never planned for things to go awry. If I could use her frustration to my advantage, I could survive this.

She'd not expected The Eight to stop Raudrich. She had no back up plan. She was nervous now, off her game, and I was just stepping up to play my own.

"What could I have possibly done? I'm a mortal, remember? I have no powers."

She screamed again and the walls seemed to shake from the power of her voice. I hoped she couldn't see my hands trembling.

"Calder must've warned them of what I would do. Damn him. I knew he couldna be trusted. He was too soft of heart. Too weak."

She stepped forward and placed her sharp, pointy nail against the main artery in my neck.

"Ye are no longer any use to me, lass. Convince me why I should make yer death painless, and perhaps I shall."

"Why would you kill me when I'm the only one left who can help free you?"

She did her best to give nothing away, but I didn't miss the slight twitch of surprise in her brow at my question.

"Free me? As ye just reminded me—ye are a mortal. There is nothing ye can do for me."

I smiled.

"Yes, there is. I don't want to die."

She was understandably skeptical.

"Ye wouldna do it, lass. Ye doona have it in ye to kill him."

"You're right. On my own, I don't have it in me. But I'm a coward, Machara, and no matter how much I care for Raudrich, I really don't want to die."

I hesitated and slowly reached up to push her hand away from my throat.

"But it doesn't matter if I don't have it in me to kill him, does it? Not when you can make sure that I follow through with my word."

When she just stared at me, mistrust in her eyes, I continued.

"Why was it that Calder brought me to you? He didn't want to. He did it because he had no choice. He did it because his oath to you prevented him from doing differently."

A light sparked in her eyes, and I could see the moment she understood.

"Ye wish to strike a bargain with me, lass?"

I nodded as I carefully formed the deal I wished to make in my mind. I couldn't misspeak a single word, and once the bargain was struck, I would have to move quickly.

"Release me from this cell, promise me that you won't harm me once you are free, and I will run Raudrich through with Calder's sword."

Her hand gripped mine in an instant and our deal was sealed.

Her eyes were sparkling with her anticipated victory as she uttered the words that sent me through to the other side of the cell bars in the span of a blink.

I moved without thought, determined to do what I knew I must before Machara had a chance to realize that I would betray her.

I ran over to where the sword had fallen.

Raudrich lay on his back, his arms spread out beside him.

My hands trembled as I lifted Calder's sword and held it above the center of Raudrich's chest.

Just as Marchara began to laugh, I plunged the sword downward with all my might, changing its direction at the last second before it pierced his skin. Rather than his heart, I ran it through his right shoulder.

When the sword's tip hit the stone floor beneath Raudrich, Machara began to scream.

She no longer had any power over me. I'd not said I would kill him. I'd only promised that I would run him through with the sword.

She cursed and wailed, but I could see in her eyes that she knew she'd been beaten.

CHAPTER 45

 hree Weeks Later

Dear Morna,

I know that you won't respond to this letter, and that's absolutely fine. I hope it finds you well all the same. This surprises no one more than me, but I just wanted to say thank you.

Thank you for all you didn't do. I can see now why you stayed away.

If you'd given me a way to get home, I might've run before I allowed myself to fall in love.

If you'd stepped in to help me with Machara, I wouldn't have learned my own strength. And if not for the book you placed in my path, Kate wouldn't have done all the research that prompted her to come here.

She's going to like it in this time, I can tell. And if the way Maddock keeps looking at her is any indication, I have a feeling we may have another romance on our hands very soon.

But you already knew that, didn't you?

"*Y*er mother is looking for ye, lass. She wishes to speak to ye before we leave for our honeymoon."

I groaned and set down the quill as Raudrich entered the bedchamber.

"How long until her cottage is finished?" Mom had been the stressed-out terror I'd known she would be from the moment she arrived.

Raudrich laughed and bent to kiss me as I walked over to him.

"A fortnight, at least. She isna so bad, really. Paton rather likes her."

"Paton doesn't like her. He likes irritating her. He gets way too much pleasure from it."

Secretly, so did I.

Raudrich rested his chin on the top of my head as I snuggled into him.

"What are ye doing, lass? Please doona tell me ye've already grown bored of yer husband and have found another man to write love letters to."

"Nothing about you bores me." I smiled and unthinkingly placed my left hand on his shoulder to pull myself up to kiss him. He winced and stepped away from me.

"Careful, lass. 'Tis still quite tender."

"You should've let them heal you with magic like they did last time."

He shook his head.

"I doona wish to be rid of this scar, lass. It reminds me of how much ye care for me. I've never had someone love me enough to stab me straight through." He paused and pointed to the writing table. "Will ye be long? I've the horse packed and ready."

"I can't wait to go away with you. I'll hurry down as fast as I can."

He kissed me until I was breathless. I knew he meant to give me a taste of what was waiting for me once we got away from the castle for our month-long respite together.

Once he was gone, I moved to finish my letter, scribbling much more quickly than before.

Raudrich is waiting for me, so I must hurry. We're about to leave on our honeymoon, but I just wanted to let you know how thankful I am for your interference in my life. I didn't know how much was missing from my life—the joy, love, adventure, and friendship. I wasn't totally sure at first, but you've converted me. I'm a fan. Although he'll never say it out loud, I'm pretty sure Marcus is, too.

Much love,

Laurel

P.S. Speaking of Marcus, can I ask you for a favor on his behalf? Since you can't seem to help yourself when it comes to setting people up, send someone Marcus' way when the time is right. He needs someone, too.

Folding the letter neatly, I sealed it with a kiss and threw it into the flames.

I could scarcely believe how much my life had changed in a matter of months.

All thanks to one meddling witch and a whole lot of love.

EPILOGUE

*M*achara's Dungeon

She could blame no one but herself. Her haste to escape had made her foolish, but she wouldn't make the same mistake again.

It was time to unearth her biggest secret.

One of her children still lived, locked away in the land of the faerie, raised by another far less powerful than she.

It was time to help the boy remember just to whom he belonged.

Soon, she'd have help in escaping.

Once she did, The Eight and all those they loved would die.

It was only a matter of time.

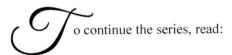

o continue the series, read:

Love Beyond Wanting
(Book 10 of Morna's Legacy Series)

READ ALL THE BOOKS IN MORNA'S LEGACY SERIES

And More to Come...

SWEET/CLEAN VERSIONS OF MORNA'S LEGACY SERIES

If you enjoy sweet/clean romances where the love scenes are left behind closed doors or if you know someone else who does, check out the new sweet/clean versions of Morna's Legacy books in the Magical Matchmaker's Legacy.

Morna's Spell

Sweet/Clean Version of *Love Beyond Time*

Morna's Secret

Sweet/Clean Version of *Love Beyond Reason*

The Conall's Magical Yuletide

Sweet/Clean Version of *A Conall Christmas*

Morna's Accomplice

Sweet/Clean Version of *Love Beyond Measure*

Jeffrey's Only Wish

Sweet/Clean Version of *In Due Time*

Morna's Rogue

Sweet/Clean Version of *Love Beyond Compare*

Morna's Ghost

Sweet/Clean Version of *Love Beyond Dreams*

SUBSCRIBE TO BETHANY'S MAILING LIST

When you sign up for my mailing list, you will be the first to know about new releases, upcoming events, and contests. You will also get sneak peeks into books and have opportunities to participate in special reader groups and occasionally get codes for free books.

Just go to my website (www.bethanyclaire.com) and click the Mailing List link in the header. I can't wait to connect with you there.

LETTER TO READERS

Dear Reader,

I hope you enjoyed *Love Beyond Words*. The next book in the series is *Love Beyond Wanting*. Order your copy today.

As an author, I love feedback from readers. You are the reason that I write, and I love hearing from you. If you would like to connect, there are several ways you can do so. You can reach out to me on Facebook or on Twitter or visit my Pinterest boards. If you want to read excerpts from my books, listen to audiobook samples, learn more about me, and find some cool downloadable files related to the books, visit my website.

The best way to stay in touch is to subscribe to my newsletter. Go to my website and click the Mailing List link in the header. If you don't hear from me regularly, please check your spam folder or junk mail to make sure my messages aren't ending up there. Please set up your email to allow my messages through to you so you never miss a new book, a chance to win great prizes or a possible appearance in your area.

Finally, if you enjoyed this book, I would appreciate it so much if you would recommend it to your friends and family. And if you would please take time to review it on Goodreads and/or your favorite retailer site, it would be a great help. Reviews can be tough to come by these days, and you, the reader, have the power to make or break a book.

Thank you so much for reading my stories. I hope you choose to journey with me through the other books in the series.

All my best,

Bethany

ABOUT THE AUTHOR

BETHANY CLAIRE is a USA Today bestselling author of swoon-worthy, Scottish romance and time travel novels. Bethany loves to immerse her readers in worlds filled with lush landscapes, hunky Scots, lots of magic, and happy endings.

She has two ornery fur-babies, plays the piano every day, and loves Disney and yoga pants more than any twenty-something really should. She is most creative after a good night's sleep and the perfect cup of tea. When not writing, Bethany travels as much as she possibly can, and she never leaves home without a good book to keep her company.

If you want to read more about Bethany or if you're curious about when her next book will come out, please visit her website at: www.bethanyclaire.com, where you can sign up to receive email notifications about new releases.

ACKNOWLEDGMENTS

This book was a bit of a departure. We've traveled to a brand new place, we're dealing with new magical beings, and the overall feel is just a little different. I can honestly say this might be my new favorite. I had so much fun with these characters, but as per usual, I really pushed the deadline with this one, and I have several wonderful people to thank for helping me get this ready in a crunch.

Karen Corboy, Elizabeth Halliday, Johnetta Ivey, and Vivian Nwankpah, thank you ladies so, so much for your help and your encouragement. You're so much more than team members, you are beloved friends. Thank you for your time and work.

Mom, I feel like we've finally gotten in a groove that works really, really well. Thanks for adjusting and putting up with my frustrating writing habits. Without you, these books would never get done. I love you.

Printed in Great Britain
by Amazon